PENGUIN MODERN CLASSICS

The Encyclopedia of the Dead

DANILO KIŠ (1935–1989) was born in Subotica, a town in northern Yugoslavia. His father Eduard was an assimilated Hungarian Jew by origin, who worked as a railway inspector. His mother Milica came from Montenegro, where she was raised in Eastern Orthodox Christianity. Danilo and his sister Danica (b. 1932) were baptized in the Orthodox Church as a defence against the anti-Semitic persecution that was spreading across central Europe. Eduard, having narrowly survived a pogrom against Serbs and Jews in 1942, took his wife and children to live in his native village in Hungary. They survived there in penury until 1944, when Germany occupied Hungary and 437,000 Jews were deported to Auschwitz, including Eduard with his siblings and cousins. Milica took her children home to Montenegro in 1947. After her death in 1950, Danilo's uncle and aunt looked after him. Danilo went to university in Belgrade, becoming Yugoslavia's first graduate in World Literature. Except for periods of employment as a lector at French universities, he remained in Belgrade until 1979, when he settled in Paris. Two short novels (*The Garret* and *Psalm 44*) were published in 1962. *Garden, Ashes* (1965) and *Hourglass* (1972) treat his and his family's experiences during the war. *A Tomb for Boris Davidovich* (1976) is a cycle of stories about revolution and violence. Its publication in English in 1978 brought a measure of international fame. His last book was a collection of stories, *The Encyclopedia of the Dead* (1983). Diagnosed with lung cancer in 1986, he died in Paris and is buried in Belgrade. He was married to Mirjana Miočinović between 1962 and 1981; his partner in the last decade was Pascale Delpech. Comprising poems, plays and essays as well as fiction, his complete works run to ten volumes. At the latest count, his writing has been translated into 42 languages. More information is available at www.danilokis.org.

MARK THOMPSON was born in Sheffield and lives in Oxford. He has published two books about the end of Yugoslavia (*A Paper House* and *Forging War*). His history of Italy in the First World War (*The White War*, 2008) was awarded the Hessell-Tiltman Prize by English PEN and shortlisted for the Orwell Prize and the Duff Cooper Prize. His biography of Danilo Kiš, *Birth Certificate* (2013), was a finalist in the category of biography for the National Book Critics Circle Award. He has translated fiction from French, Italian and Croatian. He was an information officer in the biggest peacekeeping mission deployed by the United Nations (UNPROFOR, with approx. 44,000 personnel), and the political officer in the smallest mission (UNMOP, with 28 personnel). He works in London for the Open Society Foundations, and teaches doctoral candidates in Oxford and Norwich.

DANILO KIŠ

The Encyclopedia of the Dead

Translated by Michael Henry Heim

Revised and with an Introduction by Mark Thompson

PENGUIN BOOKS

PENGUIN CLASSICS

UK | USA | Canada | Ireland | Australia
India | New Zealand | South Africa

Penguin Books is part of the Penguin Random House group of companies
whose addresses can be found at global.penguinrandomhouse.com.

First published in Serbo-Croatian as *Enciklopedija mrtvih* 1983
Published in Penguin Books 1991
Published with a new Introduction in Penguin Classics 2015
001

Text copyright © Danilo Kiš and Globus, 1983
Translation copyright © Farrar, Straus and Giroux, 1989
Introduction copyright © Mark Thompson, 2015

The moral right of the author has been asserted

Portions of this book have appeared, in slightly different form, in *Antaeus*,
Cross Currents, *Formations*, *Harper's* and *Partisan Review*. The title story, in
a different translation, appeared in *The New Yorker*.

Set in 11.25/14 pt Minion Pro
Typeset by Jouve (UK), Milton Keynes
Printed in Great Britain by Clays Ltd, St Ives plc

A CIP catalogue record for this book is available from the British Library

ISBN: 978–0–141–39698–9

www.greenpenguin.co.uk

Contents

Ma rage d'aimer donne sur la mort comme une fenêtre sur la cour.

GEORGES BATAILLE

Introduction: Danilo Kiš and pocket-sized novels

Danilo Kiš was a maker of fiction who distrusted fantasy, a dreamer obsessed with politics and historical truth. Standing over six feet tall, slim and blue-eyed under a mane of hair, with a smoky baritone voice raised in conversation or song, he cut a dramatic figure. His credo as an artist was, however, austere and even self-effacing. The work is everything; what it fails to communicate can hardly be discussed. In his lifetime, Kiš came to personify liberal pluralist values that stuck in the throats of communists and nationalists alike. Since his death in 1989, his books have survived the wars that destroyed his country and even his language to find an audience around the world. *The Encyclopedia of the Dead* has been translated into twenty-five languages including Basque, Norwegian, Thai and, most recently, Korean.

Danilo Kiš was born in 1935 at the northern edge of Yugoslavia, a multinational state established after the First World War as a unitary kingdom. His father Eduard was an assimilated Hungarian Jew by origin who worked as a railway inspector, while his mother Milica was an Orthodox Christian from Montenegro, beside the Adriatic Sea. As the offspring of this union, Kiš called himself an 'ethnographic rarity'.

At the end of 1938, with anti-Semitism looming across central Europe, Danilo's parents took the wise precaution of baptizing him and his sister Danica in the Serbian Orthodox Church. In spring 1941, war brought Hungarian fascist occupation of the northern territory. Early in 1942 the occupiers carried out a pogrom in Novi Sad, where the Kiš family lived. Eduard was taken away but the children were spared. By fluke, Eduard was released; he then decided the family would be safer in his native village in south-western Hungary. There they scraped by until German forces overran Hungary in 1944. Eduard was deported to Auschwitz alongside his relatives. Milica and her children remained in the village, waiting, but this time Eduard did not return. In 1947 Milica's brother traced the survivors and took them back to Yugoslavia, which had been remade as a communist federation that possessed – as the quip went – seven frontiers, six republics, five nationalities, four languages, three religions, two alphabets and one dictator: Josip Broz Tito. It was Europe's most diverse country.

Danilo learned his native tongue again as a schoolboy in Montenegro. By the time he went to university in Belgrade in 1954, his mother had died and his sister had married and moved away. Writing became his mainstay, a realm where he could turn loss into literature, mastering through narrative the brutal collisions that had blighted his childhood. His first books of note, *Garden, Ashes* (1965) and *Hourglass* (1972), transposed his childhood experiences into fiction. History in Kiš's writing has something like the status that Nature had for painters in earlier centuries. It is the element where fiction encounters the real world, the guarantor of proportion and value. History offers the stability of truth as well as the infinity of approaches to that truth. It is the juggernaut that killed his father, but it is also the history of literature itself – a living record and resource.

History limits the interest that mere imagination can arouse. Angela Carter noted this when she reviewed the book in 1989: 'Truth is always stranger than fiction, because the human imagination is finite while the world is not'. This is why Kiš's idea of literary perfection was 'a work that, after the first time round, can be read like an encyclopedia'. A work so charged with knowledge, so accessible yet seductively structured that its riches yield themselves little by little. (Joyce's *Ulysses* was the gold standard, a great novel that was also a great manual of technique.) Fiction has to reckon with history, not shun or flatter it. This elusive middle way opens only to mastery of form. Kiš loved the *mise en abyme*, fiction that draws reflexively on literature to create vertiginous effects: stories within stories, where reading, writing and interpretation are intrinsic to the plot. The two best examples in this book are 'The Encyclopedia of the Dead' and 'Red Stamps with Lenin's Head', which happened to be Kiš's favourites.

After *Hourglass*, Kiš turned to the crimes of Stalinism and the delusions of its foreign supporters. *A Tomb for Boris Davidovich* (1976) was meant to be a political shocker and it succeeded as such, but the additional scandal it provoked was of another kind: he came under attack for plagiarism from powerful figures on Belgrade's literary scene. Kiš retaliated, and over several months traded blows with his detractors in the press. He developed his argument at length in *The Anatomy Lesson* (1978), fusing literary theory with scathing polemic, which led to a criminal defamation case. By the time the court found in his favour in 1979, Kiš's private life was falling apart. His marriage with Mirjana Miočinović had weathered various infidelities, but he was now embroiled in a long affair with a former student, who was translating his fiction into French. Amid these strains, Kiš accepted the position of lector at the University of Lille. By the time he moved into a tiny flat in the tenth arrondissement of Paris at the end of summer 1979, he and Mirjana were estranged.

So, when he wrote *The Encyclopedia of the Dead*, Kiš was unusually isolated. In his mid-forties, expatriated, financially precarious, childless and separated from his partner of some twenty-five years, he was alone with his vocation. After Penguin published *A Tomb for Boris Davidovich* in 1980 to acclaim, he might have launched a career as an émigré dissident denouncing communism, but he was too much his own man, averse to political capture and proud of not repeating himself. At his trestle desk in Paris, he found himself writing pastiche fables and historical probes, inventing or elaborating biographies, reworking timeless legends and also incidents from his own life.

When sifting through these stories for his next book, he excluded those that were recognizably personal and contemporary.* The resulting collection shines by any standard, fit company for Flaubert's *Trois Contes* and Borges's *Ficciones*. Breadth of allusion, sombre unity of theme around the operatic pairing of love and death, miniaturist precision of style, and variety of voice combine to achieve what Kiš most admired: the grace of form. Every detail, every angle and the slightest shift between lyrical flight and granular wisdom add meaning. Objects hover on the brink of enlarging into archetypes or allegories of themselves, without losing their unique dimensions.

Kiš had worked out his thoughts about the short story a few years earlier, in an essay called 'Novels for the Palm of Your Hand'. The European cataclysm from 1914 to 1945 had 'disintegrated' the traditional novel – the sort that uses omniscient narration and free indirect speech to blend with readers' inward accounts of their own experience. But the post-war novel had risen from the ashes and proven that it was still 'the confluence of the entire *condition humaine*, the seismograph of the Hegelian world spirit'.

The short story, on the other hand, was languishing 'in a state of permanent stagnation, with signs of imminent expiry'. Writers had nobody else to blame; they had let themselves be

---

* These would be published posthumously in *The Lute and the Scars*.

led astray by Maupassant, Chekhov and O. Henry – who preceded the cataclysm – into swallowing the idea that 'the totality of the world and of experience' could be revealed in 'a slice of life'. Kiš defined this as the genre of story that

signals a presentiment of higher laws by means of a fragment, an *image*; that creates a complete picture of the world and time, a 'totality of experience' through a single gesture, an insignificant day in the life of an insignificant character, by means of deduction (in terms of ontology) and induction (in terms of literary technique).

This kind of story was doomed to fail, Kiš argued, because human meaning after the cataclysm had disintegrated along with the traditional novel, and for the same reason. It could no longer be summoned by an image or a gesture.

For this reason *stories* are more and more becoming *short novels* . . . Nothing is supremely meaningful and nothing is meaningless: descriptions of things and topics, proffered with cold objectivity, carry the same significance as the spiritual condition of heroes in tales of old; they are the cells of a single organism; every topic – like every pore on the hero's skin – is a sort of micro-organism which bears witness to the malady and crisis of the world in which he, my hero (if there is one at all), lives.

He ends by quoting the 'classic and only adequate' definition of the genre, by the Russian formalist critic Boris Eikhenbaum:

The story is a problem through posing a single equation with one unknown; the novel is a problem involving various rules and soluble with the aid of a whole system of equations with various unknowns, where the intermediary steps are more important than the final answer.

A story should, then, differ from a novel only in the number of elements or variables that it puts into play and in the unanimity of its development. Brevity was no excuse for inert form.

For Kiš, the route to Eikhenbaum's ideal lay through the global literary heritage (he was, after all, Yugoslavia's first graduate in World Literature), steering by the star of his childhood love for the folk poetry he had heard on his mother's knee. In *The Encyclopedia of the Dead*, this heritage encompasses Gnostic myths, a Koranic legend, an anti-Semitic tract, Russian poetry and the bibliographical fantasies of Borges. With these and other inspirations, some of them intimate, Kiš framed stories that drew on his perennial concerns – love, persecution, delusion, complicity, death. The legacy of Balkan folk poetry is felt in the emotional primary colours and the impersonal, unpossessive handling of the material.

The first story, 'Simon Magus', is set in Palestine a few years after the crucifixion of Christ.* The trackways are dotted with 'gentle, blue-eyed young men' who preach on wobbly barrels and flare with rage when contradicted. Simon wanders from village to village, denouncing Christ's followers as charlatans and their god as 'a tyrant, a vindictive tyrant'. Encountering the disciple Peter, Simon is challenged to perform a miracle.

---

* Simon Magus figured centrally in the heretical doctrines known as Gnosticism that spread around the eastern Roman Empire in the first centuries after Christ. Gnostic doctrines held that secret knowledge (*gnosis*) could liberate people from the material world and its irremediable evil. Our souls are divine sparks trapped in this world. Gnosis can release these sparks and reunite them with their unknowable source. The entity at the origin of all things was the unnameable father, and the final emanation of the divine being was Sophia, who conceived a desire to know the father without the father's awareness. This desire created a veil in the divine realm; the shadow of this veil became the material world. The early Gnostics included many Jews for whom the destruction of the temple in Jerusalem in AD 70 marked the failure of their god.

He declares that he will fly up to the sky. He flaps his arms, stays earthbound, is mocked, and redoubles his efforts. Concentrating on random examples of earthly suffering, Simon soars into the air. As he dwindles to a dot below the clouds, 'Peter stood petrified' at the prospect of metaphysical pluralism: if what he witnesses is real, 'then His miracles and the truth of the Christian faith were *but one of the truths of this world* and not the sole truth, then the world was a mystery and truth an illusion'. But God answers Peter's prayer; Simon plunges full speed down to earth; his grisly death vindicates the 'tyrant'.*

Kiš was fascinated by Gnosticism. It corresponded to his sense that the world was tyrannized by force and that life might be redeemed by knowledge, or made tolerable at least. In 'Simon Magus', defiance of power is brave but doomed; the glimpse of pluralism is expunged. Kiš was pipped for a prize by a Serbian poet in 1984 because one of the jurors suspected that 'Simon Magus' was meant to foretell the collapse of communism. If the story carries a political meaning, it concerns the vanity of dissidence; Simon should not have accepted Peter's arrogant dare. But the story is also about the enchantment of reading, and art's relationship to history and force. Art's triumphs are transient, absolute in their way but incapable of vying with faith or ideology. Fiction builds its airy castles only to disperse them. 'My definition of literature', Kiš once said, 'is an attempt at a global vision of reality and its simultaneous destruction'.

The second story, 'Last Respects', elaborates a tiny scene from a once-famous memoir by Richard Krebs, alias Jan

---

* Although his English was rudimentary, a meticulous sense for language led Kiš to correct Michael Henry Heim when he rendered '*Petar se petrificirao*' as 'Peter turned to stone'. Paraphrase is a snare for translators.

Valtin. The sailor and revolutionary Bandura grieves passionately for the good-hearted prostitute Mariette; he and his followers heap her grave with flowers liberated from the parks and bourgeois gardens of Hamburg. More than an occasion for mild anti-communist satire, Mariette's interest lies in her peculiar integrity ('she *was* a harbour whore') and her merging of uniqueness and universality; nobody else was like her, and she was available to all – like a true work of art. Yet death means complete extinction: 'for a moment, he catches a mental glimpse of her smile, a shadow of her face, but soon they too dissolve'. Art aspires to a longer duration.

This desolate outcome is qualified by the next story, which is the book's masterpiece. 'The Encyclopedia of the Dead' is narrated by an unnamed female academic. Seeking distraction from her grief after the death of her father, she accepts an invitation to Stockholm, where one evening her host leads her to the Royal Library. In a room 'like a dungeon', filled with volumes of an immense encyclopedia, she passes the night reading the entry about her father, which tells his life in miraculous detail and a matchless style, from birth to death. 'Each item has its own paragraph, each period its own poetic essence and metaphor.'

The encyclopedia is produced by 'a religious organization or sect whose democratic program stresses an egalitarian vision of the world of the dead', an 'odd caste of erudites' with 'members all over the world', who 'believe in the miracle of biblical resurrection and they compile their vast catalogue in preparation for that moment'. Only people who do not feature in any other encyclopedia are admitted. 'The principle is clear, yet the erudition, the need to record it all, everything a human life is made of, is enough to take one's breath away.' The point of the encyclopedia is its inclusiveness. The narrator marvels at her father's biography: 'The countryside of his native region is rendered so vividly that as I read, or rather flew over the lines and paragraphs, I felt I was in the heart of it'. Kiš is describing any reader's ideal experience. At the end, the narrator reveals that the story has been a dream: 'I awoke drenched in sweat'.

Kiš called the story a 'condensed novel' about 'an ordinary Yugoslav man'. It was an elegy for his country when it still had a decade to live. But it is also much more than this. The English critic Chris Miller hails the story as 'a Borgesian fantasy, a celebration of life, a meta-fiction on the impossible ideal of fiction, and a political ideal. The experience of reading the titular *Encyclopedia of the Dead* is, naturally, revealed to be a dream. But in the short story of that name, the dream is all but fulfilled'. For Julia Creet, the story is about hypermnesia, 'the dream of complete knowledge'. For historian Angus Calder, it 'speaks for all the forgotten and anonymous dead' in twentieth-century Europe. The story feels as universal as that, while it takes its place in a strain of half-mystical Jewish writing about redemption by narrative – what Walter Benjamin called 'honouring the memory of the nameless'.

The Bosnian American author Aleksandar Hemon sees the story as Kiš's highest achievement in reconciling poetics and politics. 'The absolute value of the individual is the crucial premise of Kiš's poetics as also of his politics', Hemon says, and the form of the story follows from this radical humanist premise. 'History as the sum of human destinies or the totality of ephemeral events is a different concept from national history or the history of nations, including nationalist history. As soon as an individual life is organized on the basis of ethno-national historical hierarchies, that life is swallowed up by nationalist ideology. And the ideology of nationalism, like the ideology of communism, is a story about a collective, never about an individual. The collision between Kiš's poetics or politics and the dominant concept of history in this part of the world is perfectly clear.'

The story is dedicated to his then-wife Mirjana, whose dream about her father Đuro the year after his death in 1979 had provided the seed. 'The dream was very simple and I remember every detail to this day', she remembers.

I am speaking with my father, who is dead, telling him how I am going to show him what we have done for him since he died. Together we are watching the following sight, as if in a cinema: white marble headstones in a grassy clearing, all the same and practically identical to the marble slab (50 × 50 cm) on the tomb where my father's ashes are buried. A copse of trees can be seen in the background. I tell my father that we buried him in Sweden. He considers this and says 'Very well, but why Sweden?' To which I say 'Because that's where the great encyclopedia is with entries for everyone who has died'. Then I open an enormous book and show him the columns that are devoted to him, where I can see – and I tell him so – an enormous flower that he had painted. Then I wake up.

She told her dream to Kiš, who was deeply impressed. (He had already moved to Paris but they were not yet divorced.) He said a day or two later that he wanted to write a story about it. She encouraged him, listing the biographical facts about her father in a letter. We have Mirjana's word that Kiš's portrait of 'D.M.' is true to life, but what matters to us is the story's ring of truth, its power of conviction. This power rests, finally, on Kiš's skill in soliciting the expectation of fantasy and then withholding fulfilment; he keeps the possibility and its denial in play almost to the end. When the story's first translator, Ammiel Alcalay, offered it to the *New Yorker* magazine, the fiction editor was enthusiastic but wondered if Kiš might wish to alter the ending so the narrative would not be revealed as a dream. Kiš was indignant. 'I don't write so-called fantastic tales. I am a realistic writer'. He would not, he meant, insult his readers by assuming they might be induced to believe in the impossible encyclopedia, or humiliate himself by the attempt. Dreams, on the other hand, are real.

In 'The Legend of the Sleepers', Kiš adapts scriptural archaisms and incantatory rhythms to reimagine the story of seven Roman noblemen, converts to Christianity in the court of pagan emperor Decius. Punished for their faith by immurement in a cave, the seven fall into a miraculous sleep which lasts two centuries. They awaken into a changed world, ruled by the Christian emperor Theodosius. Amid celebrations at their return, the sleepers tell their story and bless the emperor, then pass peacefully into real sleep and death. The invitation in Borges's story 'Averroës' Search' ('Let us imagine that someone *shows* a story instead of telling it – the story of the seven sleepers of Ephesus, say.') may have been Kiš's cue to evoke the impossible experience of the sleeper Dionysius. The return of sensation to stone-like limbs, the 'crimson flame' of sunlight, the swirling confusion of dream and reality, the frightening hubbub of the crowd: these are presented with barely a hint of explanation. The final vindication of faith is omitted; Kiš's sleepers simply find themselves back in the cave, objects not subjects of their untellable tale.

'The Mirror of the Unknown' was Kiš's only venture into the supernatural. A chronicle of death foreseen, it tells of a Jewish family in mid-nineteenth century Hungary. A father goes on a journey with two of his daughters, leaving behind his wife and youngest girl. That night, the girl at home dreams that the three travellers have been killed. At that very moment, they are attacked and murdered by thieves. The story appears to meditate on the slaughter of Hungarian Jews in 1944 and the futility of seeking psychological explanations for such evil. When the murderers are caught with their blood-stained loot, they admit their guilt and ask for a priest to hear their confession: a request as senseless as the crime. A remark that Kiš underlined in a book by Bruno Bettelheim provides a gloss: 'Contrary to general belief, evil is neither tragic nor romantic; most of the time, it is banal'.

Set among the Jews of old Prague, 'The Story of the Master and the Disciple' tells how a renowned scholar helps a young admirer to improve his manuscript. So well does Ben Haas succeed in making the 'Appearance of Substance' resemble 'Substance' that other scholars are convinced Yeshua Krochal's book is the real thing. The disciple, who has destroyed all evidence of the Master's help, then denounces him, 'using gossip and slander in a manner that showed him to be not entirely without talent'. The Master has added to the sum of deceit in the world. Vanity is to blame: 'Leaning over the abyss, not even he could resist the vain pleasure of trying to fill it with Sense'. In fine, the demands of art and those of morality cannot be reconciled. This is the only story in *The Encyclopedia of the Dead* that was written before Kiš left Belgrade, and according to the Postscript (added to the book to forestall renewed accusations of plagiarism), the disciple was modelled on a real person in Belgrade whom Kiš had helped and who would repay the debt by joining the campaign against *Boris Davidovich*, 'using gossip and slander'. So the story turned out to be prophetic. It feels cramped, however, its wit too Borgesian, as if held hostage to its origins in a private vexation.

'Pro Patria Mori' is about the genesis of political myth in a welter of ambiguity, betrayal and misconception. The young rebel's mother deceives her son so that his seeming courage on the scaffold will save family honour. Myth is the stock-in-trade of history, which has no conscience. For conscience is measured by scrupulous and accountable form, connecting the producers of narrative with its consumers in an ethical relationship. The story ends with a series of dicta so plangent and quotable that people quickly forgot they were meant in part as pastiche: 'History is written by the victors. Traditions are woven by the people. Writers fantasise. Only death is certain'.

The tension between history and literature recurs in 'The Book of Kings and Fools', a fictionalized account of the origins of the *Protocols of the Elders of Zion*. As the most successful and deadly of all literary hoaxes, the *Protocols* revealed a supposed Jewish plot for world domination. They became a staple of Nazi propaganda and are still cited in the Arab world as an authentic and authoritative document. No other subject united so many of Kiš's obsessions: the nexus of fiction and atrocity, the mysterious byways of plagiarism, the persistence of anti-Semitic prejudice, the wilful credulity of most readers. Above all, the career of the *Protocols* confirmed Angela Carter's axiom about truth and fiction. As Kiš liked to tell interviewers, nothing is more fantastic than reality.

The last story in the book, 'Red Stamps with Lenin's Head' was also the last to be written and the only one that he did not share with Mirjana before publication. It takes the form of a letter to an unnamed scholar from a woman who also remains nameless. The letter concerns Mendel Osipovich, a Russian Jewish poet who wrote in Yiddish between the 1920s and the 1940s. The woman claims to have been the poet's secret muse; as such, she can answer the question posed by the scholar during a recent lecture (which she attended incognito): 'What has become of Mendel Osipovich's correspondence?' She alone can solve this mystery, by recounting the story of their love. This culminates in her discovery that, after many years together, Osipovich had become intimate with a younger woman who was translating his poems into Russian. 'I believe

I could have forgiven him an infidelity of the flesh – with poets as with gods, anything is forgivable. But the fact that he wrote to the young woman about his poetry, his soul, the mysterious sources of his inspiration . . . that, sir, is what shattered me, shook my very being'. She fetches the packet of his letters and destroys them. What nobody else knew at the time is that Mirjana had destroyed Kiš's letters to her, in a fit of hopeless rage, on the day of their divorce in July 1981. Having lost her, he was ready to write about her, just as – having emigrated in 1979 – he had written about Yugoslavia in 'The Encyclopedia of the Dead'. In each case, an interval of a year and a half elapsed between loss and composition: the pace of his creative metabolism.

The book appeared in 1983 as the last volume of his collected works. Still smarting from the accusations against *Boris Davidovich*, Kiš broke with his habit of launching new work with a round of explanatory interviews. The critics had to fend for themselves. Perhaps as a result, the reviews were few in number and rather offhand. But there were other reasons too for this reception. *The Encyclopedia of the Dead* emerged into a country that no longer knew what it stood for. Tito's long-anticipated death in 1980 had left a besetting and insidious sense of uncertainty. Communism in Europe was slowly eroding, but liberals in Yugoslavia were weak against the nationalist intellectuals who fanned historical resentments against neighbouring peoples. So the 1980s saw the creation or resurrection of national myths, drawing on the traditionalism and authoritarianism that were rooted in Yugoslav society.

In this febrile climate, Kiš's tales of deception and manipulation, false prophesy, conspiracy, the helplessness of mind against mindless violence and the links between language and cruelty could not have been more apt: a handful of counter-myths, so well crafted and packed with matter that they outlast the political madness and private misery which informed them.

Excepting *The Anatomy Lesson*, Kiš never hurried to start a new book. By 1986, he was mulling over an idea for a novel about a (real) sixteenth-century Sephardic poet who fled from persecution in Portugal to Italy and then to Dubrovnik. At the end of that year, before he had written a line, Kiš was diagnosed with lung cancer. The remainder of his life was overshadowed by sickness and fear of death. In a startling interview for a Dutch newspaper, he said that his cancer had originated around about the time when he wrote 'The Encyclopedia of the Dead'. In that story, the narrator discovers that her father's fatal tumour dated from the time when he started 'painting floral patterns all over the house'; so 'his obsession with floral patterns coincided with the progress of the disease'. It followed, Kiš said, that cancer was 'a punishment for playing the creator, for competing with God'. One of his best critics, Viktória Radics, has pointed out the resemblance to Simon Magus in this despairing avowal.

The fact that Kiš wrote no more fiction after *The Encyclopedia of the Dead* has lent the book a valedictory, almost testamentary feeling. Yet this is inherent in the stories themselves, which seem to epitomize his work with definitive eloquence while moving towards a terminus, as if preparing – the Bosnian writer Miljenko Jergović has praised it in these terms – to lose the battle with silence and the impossibility of writing.

Bibliography and acknowledgements

Walter Benjamin, *Illuminations*, translated by Harry Zohn (New York: Shocken Books, 1968)

Bruno Bettelheim, *Survivre* (Paris: Robert Laffont, 1976)

Melvyn Bragg, Caroline Humfress, Alastair Logan, Martin Palmer, 'Gnosticism', *In Our Time*, BBC Radio 4, 2 May 2013, at http://www.bbc.co.uk/programmes/b01s4rhz

Angus Calder, ed., *Wars* (London: Penguin Books, 1999)

Angela Carter, 'Danilo Kis: *The Encyclopedia of the Dead*', in *Expletives Deleted. Selected Writings* (London: Chatto & Windus, 1992)

Julia Creet, 'The Archive and the Uncanny. Danilo Kiš's "Encyclopedia of the Dead" and the Fantasy of Hypermnesia', in *Lost in the Archives*, edited by Rebecca Comay, Alphabet City, no. 8 (Toronto: Alphabet City Media)

Predrag Čudić, *Saveti mladom piscu ili književna početnica* (Radio B92, 1996, Beograd)

Boris Eikhenbaum, 'O. Henry and the Theory of the Short Story' [1925], translated by I.R. Titunik (Ann Arbor: University of Michigan Press, 1968)

Miljenko Jergović in *ARS: Časopis za kniževnost, kulturu i društvena pitanja* 2009/4–5 (Montenegro)

Danilo Kiš, 'Romani na dlanu', in *Homo Poeticus* (Belgrade: BIGZ, 1995)

Danilo Kiš, *The Lute and the Scars*, translated by John K. Cox (Champaign, IL: Dalkey Archive Press, 2012)

Chris Miller, 'Dark Materials', PN *Review* 214 (November–December 2013)

Mirjana Miočinović, Vladimir Tupanjac and Aleksandar Savanović, eds, *Danilo Kiš (1935–2005). Između poetike i politike. Međunarodni skup pisaca Beograd, 15–17. jun 2005* (Belgrade: CIP, 2011)

Mirjana Miočinović, letter to M.T., 28 May 2014

Viktorija Radič [Radics Viktória], *Danilo Kiš. Život & delo i brevijar* (Belgrade: Forum pisaca, 2005)

Mark Thompson, *Birth Certificate. The Story of Danilo Kiš* (Ithaca, NY: Cornell University Press, 2013)

Jan Valtin, *Out of the Night* (New York: Alliance Book Corporation, 1941)

With thanks to Mirjana Miočinović, Muharem Bazdulj, Cecilia Stein, Vesna Domany Hardy, Ruth Pietroni and Ivana Djordjevic.

Simon Magus

1

Seventeen years after the death and miraculous resurrection of Jesus the Nazarene, a man named Simon appeared on the dusty roads that crisscross Samaria and vanish in the desert beneath the fickle sands, a man whom his disciples called the Magus and his enemies derided as 'the Borborite'. Some claimed he had come from a miserable Samarian village named Gitta, others that he was from Syria or Anatolia. It cannot be denied that he himself contributed to the confusion, answering the most innocent questions about his origins with a wave of the hand broad enough to take in both the neighboring hamlet and half the horizon.

He was brawny and of medium height, and his black curly hair had begun to thin at the top; his beard, also curly and unkempt, was flecked with gray. He had a hooked, bony nose and a sheep-like profile. One of his eyes was larger than the other, giving his face a somewhat sarcastic expression. In his left ear he wore a gold earring: a snake swallowing its tail. His waist was wound several times around with a flaxen rope, which served as a prop for his circus tricks: suddenly it would rise straight into the air, and he would scramble up it – before the spectators' wondering eyes – as he might scramble up a bean pole. Or he would tie it around the neck of a calf and then, uttering a magic formula, chop its head off with a single slice of the sword. For a moment, head and body lay severed in the desert sand, but then the miracle worker pronounced the magic formula – backwards, this time – and the head re-attached itself to the body. Picking up the rope, which had remained in the sand, he would undo the knot and wind it around his waist again, unless a member of the audience wished to verify the fiber's composition. He would then hand him one end of the stiff rope as if offering him a stick; the moment the skeptic took hold of it, it would go limp and fall to the earth, raising a cloud of dust.

He was as fluent in Greek and Coptic as he was in Aramaic and Hebrew, and knew various local dialects, though his enemies claimed he spoke each of the languages with a strong accent. Simon paid scant heed to such rumors and even gave the impression of encouraging them. He was said to be quick-witted and an excellent orator, especially when addressing disciples and followers or the crowds that flocked to hear him. 'Then his eyes would shine like stars,' said one of his disciples. 'He had the voice of a lunatic and the eye of a lecher,' one of his adversaries remarked.

Along the tangled roads leading from East to West and West to East, Simon Magus crossed paths with a great many preachers. The disciples of John and Paul – and John and Paul themselves – were then engaged in spreading the word of Jesus the Nazarene, whose memory was still alive in Palestine, Judaea, and Samaria; and Simon frequently discovered their sandal tracks at the entrance to a village. The village would be strangely peaceful at that time of day, the only noise the barking of a dog or the resonant bleating of a sheep. Then, itself very much like braying, came the distant sound of male voices, resonant and clear, though as yet not quite intelligible. They belonged to the Apostles, who, perched on wobbly barrels, were preaching the perfection of the world and of God's Creation. Simon would hide in the shade of a hovel, waiting for them to depart, and enter the village before the people had completely dispersed.

Then, surrounded by his escort, he would himself begin to preach. Worn out by the subtle reasoning of the Apostles, the crowd was less than eager to gather round. 'We've just seen off Paul and John,' they would say to him. 'We've had enough words for a year.'

'I am not an Apostle,' Simon would say. 'I am one of you. They place their hands on your heads to inspire you with the Holy Ghost; I hold out my hands to raise you up from the dust.' Whereupon he would lift his arms skywards, his wide sleeves sliding down in graceful folds to reveal a pair of beautiful white hands and the fine fingers found only among idlers and illusionists.

'They offer you eternal salvation,' Simon would go on. 'I offer you knowledge and the desert. Anyone who wants can join me.'

The people were used to every kind of wanderer from every direction, though mostly from the East – now alone, now in pairs, now accompanied by a crowd of believers. Some left their mules and camels outside the village or at the foot of the mountain or in the next valley; others arrived with an armed escort (and their sermons were more like threats or playacting); still others rode in on their mules and, without even dismounting, launched into acrobatic tricks. But for the past fifteen years or so, since the death of a certain Nazarene, the visitors had tended to be young and healthy, with carefully trimmed beards or no beards at all, and wore white cloaks, carried shepherd's staffs, and called themselves Apostles and sons of God. Their sandals were dusty from the long journey, their words so much alike they seemed to have been learned from the same book; they all referred to the same miracle, which they had themselves witnessed: the Nazarene had turned water into wine before their eyes and fed a large crowd with a few sardines. Some claimed to have seen Him rise up to the sky in a dazzling light and reach heaven like a dove. The blind, whom they brought with them as living witnesses, claimed that the light had taken away their sight but given them spiritual enlightenment.

And they all called themselves sons of God and sons of the Son of God. For a chunk of bread and a jug of wine they promised bliss and life everlasting; and when the people chased them from their doors, setting their fierce dogs upon them, the preachers threatened them with everlasting hell where their flesh would burn over a low flame like a lamb on the spit.

There were, however, fine speakers among them, men who knew how to give the suspicious crowds and the even more suspicious authorities answers to numerous complex questions concerning not only the soul but the body, animal husbandry and farming. They cured young men of pimples and advised young girls in the hygiene of preserving their virginity and bearing it more easily; they counseled the elderly about preparation for death, about what words to utter at their mortal hour and how to cross their arms to slip through the narrows leading to the light; they told mothers how to save their progeny without expensive sorcerers and potions, and how to keep their sons from going to war; they taught barren women clear and simple prayers to say three times a day on an empty stomach so that the Holy Ghost – as they called it – might make their wombs fruitful.

And they did it all for nothing, at no cost, excepting the crust of bread they gratefully accepted or the bowl of cool water they drank in small gulps, murmuring incomprehensible words. From the four corners of the earth they came, one after the other, with various customs and tongues, with beards and without, but all bearing more or less the same message, one confirming what the other proclaimed, and apart from a slight variation in detail and a few minor inconsistencies, the tale of the miracles and resurrection of the Nazarene began to gain authenticity. The people of Judaea, Samaria, and Anatolia grew accustomed to the peaceable young men in dusty sandals who crossed their hands over their chests, spoke in virginal voices, and sang with their eyes raised to heaven. They gave the young men cool water and crusts of bread, and the young men thanked them and promised them life everlasting, describing a miraculous place they would gain after death, a land where there was no desert, no sand, no snakes or spiders, only broad-fronded palms, springs with ice-cold water, grass that grew to knee-level, and above, a mild sun, nights like days and days that never ended; a land where cows grazed, goats and sheep browsed in the pastures, flowers smelled sweet all year round, spring lasted forever, where there were no crows, no eagles, only nightingales that sang all day. And so on.

This picture of the gardens of paradise, which everyone initially regarded as ridiculous and impossible (who had ever seen a place where the sun always shone and there was no pain or death?) – this picture the gentle, blue-eyed young men evoked with such conviction, such inspiration, that people came to believe them. When a lie is repeated long enough, people start believing it. Because people need faith. Many young men donned long-laced sandals and set off with them. Some returned to their villages after a year or two, others after ten years. They returned exhausted from their long journeys, their beards speckled with white. They spoke softly now too, their hands crossed over their loins. They spoke of His miracles, of His teaching, they preached His strange laws, scorned the pleasures of the flesh, dressed modestly, ate moderately, and used both hands to raise the chalice to their lips when drinking wine. Yet if someone contradicted them, if someone cast doubt on their teaching and His miracles, if someone – woe unto him! – questioned the life everlasting and the gardens of paradise, then they would fly into a sudden rage. They would describe the tortures of eternal expiation with vigorous and violent words, menacing and fiery words. 'May the gods keep you,' a pagan wrote, 'from their evil tongues and imprecations.'

They knew how to win over skeptics with flattery and promises, bribes and threats; and the more their power spread and their followers increased, the stronger and more arrogant they grew. They blackmailed families, sowed discord in the minds of individuals, hatched plots against anyone who expressed the slightest mistrust of their doctrine. They had their own firebrands and rabble-rousers, their own secret tribunals at which they pronounced maledictions and sentences, burned the writings of their enemies, and cast anathemas on the heads of recalcitrants. People joined them in ever-increasing numbers because they rewarded the faithful and punished the rebellious.

It was at this time that Simon, called the Magus, made his appearance.

Simon preached that the God of the Apostles was a tyrant and that a tyrant could not be God to thinking men. Their God – Jehovah, Elohim – abominates mankind, chokes it, slaughters it, visits pestilences and wild beasts upon it, serpents and tarantulas, lions and tigers, thunder and lightning, plagues, leprosy, syphilis, tempests and gales, droughts and floods, nightmares and sleeplessness, the sorrows of youth and the impotence of age. He has allotted our blessed ancestors a place in the gardens of paradise, but deprived them of the sweetest fruit, the only one that man deserves, the only one that distinguishes him from the dog, the camel, the ass, and the monkey – the knowledge of good and evil.

'And when our unfortunate ancestor, driven by curiosity, wished to seize that fruit, what did their Elohim, your Elohim, the Just, the Great, the All-Powerful – what did he do then? Eh?' Simon shouted, teetering on the wobbly barrel. 'You know very well. (Your apostles – his servants and slaves – tell you in their sermons day after day.) He chased him off like a leper, a pariah, chased him mercilessly, with a fiery sword. And why? Because he is a God of animosity, of hatred and jealousy. In place of freedom he preaches slavery, in place of pleasure deprivation, in place of knowledge dogma... O people of Samaria, has not your vindictive God destroyed your houses? Has he not inflicted drought and locusts upon your fields? Has he not turned out dozens of your leprous neighbors? Did he not, only a year ago, lay waste to your village with a terrible plague? What kind of God is he, what kind of justice is his – for your apostles call him just – if he continues even now to wreak his vengeance on you for a so-called sin committed by distant ancestors? What kind of justice is his if he visits plagues, thunder and lightning, pestilence, sorrow, and misfortune upon you for no other reason than that your ancestors, driven by curiosity, by that living fire which engenders knowledge, dared to pluck the apple? No, people of Samaria, he is no God; he is an avenger, he is a brigand, an outlaw, who with his angelic hosts – armed to the teeth, armed with fiery swords and poisoned arrows – stands in your path. When your figs ripen, he sends down a blight upon them; and when your olives ripen, he sends down a storm to tear them from the trees and hail to pound them into the dirt and turn them to mud; when your sheep bring forth a lamb, he visits a plague upon them or wolves or tigers to devastate the fold;

and when you have a child, he visits convulsions upon it to cut short its life. What kind of God is he, what kind of justice is his if he does all this? No, that is not God, that is not the One who is in heaven, that is not Elohim; that is someone else. For Elohim the Creator of heaven and earth, of man and woman, of every fowl of the air and everything that creepeth upon the earth, the Creator of every living thing, the One who raised up the mountains above the seas, the One who created the seas and the rivers and the oceans, the green grasses and the shade of the palm tree, sun and rain, air and fire – *that* is Elohim, the God of justice. And the one whose teachings Peter and John and Paul and their disciples have taught you – he is a brigand and a murderer. And all that John and Paul, James and Peter tell you about him and his kingdom – hear, O people of Samaria! – is a lie. Their chosen land is a lie, their God a lie, their miracles false. They lie, because their God, to whom they swear allegiance, is false; they lie incessantly and, having thus entered into a great maelstrom of lies, no longer even realize they are lying. Where everyone lies, no one lies; where everything is lies, nothing is a lie. The kingdom of heaven, the kingdom of justice is a lie. Every attribute of their God is a lie. That he is righteous – a lie. Truth-loving – a lie. One and Only – a lie. Immortal – a lie. Their scriptures are false because they promise lies; they promise paradise, and paradise is a lie because it is in their hands, because they are the ones who stand at the gates of paradise, their angels with fiery swords and their judges with false scales.'

The people listened to him with indifference and mistrust, as a crowd listens to demagogues – seeking hidden meanings behind obscure words. For they were accustomed to hearing the authorities, the Pharisees, men with power, use sweet-sounding promises to conceal wiles, threats, and extortions, and expected this man, too, to declare his intentions, to state at last why he had come, to give the reason for his empty words, his vague and confusing prattle. That is why they kept listening. And because they hoped he would cap his muddled remarks with an acrobatic trick or a miracle.

'The kingdom of heaven rests on a foundation of lies,' Simon continued, staring into the merciless sun, 'and its roof has two slopes: white lies and black lies. Their scriptures are composed of false words and mysterious laws, and each law is a lie: ten laws, ten lies. . . It is not enough that their Elohim is a tyrant, a vindictive tyrant, and as cross as a crotchety old man; no, they want everyone to venerate him, to fall at his feet, to think of nothing else but him! To call him, that tyrant, the One and Only, All-Powerful, and Righteous God. And to submit to him alone! Who are they, O people of Samaria, these charlatans who come to you and fill your ears with lies and false promises? They are people who have secured his mercy for themselves and wish you to submit without a murmur, to suffer all the trials of existence – torments, pestilences, quakes, floods, plagues – without cursing him. Why else would he forbid you to take his name in vain? They are lies, all lies, I tell you! The things you hear from Peter and Paul, the white lies and the black lies of his disciples – they are all one big, dreadful hoax! Whence: thou shalt not kill! Killing is what he does, their One and Only, All-Powerful, and Righteous God! He is the one who smites infants in their cradles and mothers in childbirth and toothless old men! Killing is his vocation. Whence: thou shalt not kill! Leave the killing to him and his! They are the only ones called to it! They are destined to be wolves, you to be sheep! You must give yourselves up to their laws!. . . Whence: thou shalt not commit adultery, that they may carry off the flower of thy womanhood. And whence: thou shalt not covet thy neighbor's goods, for thou hast no reason to envy him. They demand everything of you – soul and body, spirit and thought – and give you promises in exchange; for your current submission and your current prayers and your current silence they give you a crazy quilt of false promises: they promise you the future, a future that does not exist. . .'

Simon did not notice, or merely pretended not to notice, that the people had dispersed and that his only remaining audience consisted of those who called themselves his disciples. All the while, his faithful companion Sophia had been wiping the sweat from his forehead and passing him a pitcher of water, which had turned lukewarm even though she had kept it deep in the sand.

Sophia was a small woman of about thirty, with thick hair and dark eyes like sloes. Over her bright, translucent cloak she wore colorful silk scarves, probably purchased in India. Simon's disciples described her as the epitome of wisdom and mature womanly beauty, while the Christian pilgrims spread all sorts of rumors about her; namely, that she was a flirt, a tramp, a tease, a hussy, and an impostor who had found grace in the eyes of her impostor of a companion in a Syrian brothel. Simon never denied it. Her former life as a slave and concubine served him as an obvious example, example and lesson, of Jehovah's brutality and the cruelty of this world. That Fallen Angel, that Stray Sheep, he maintained, was merely a victim of God's brutality, a Pure Soul imprisoned in human flesh, her spirit having migrated for centuries from vessel to vessel, from body to body, from shadow to shadow. She was Lot's daughter and she was Rachel and she was Fair Helen. (In other words, the Greeks and the barbarians had admired a shadow and shed blood over a phantom!) Her most recent incarnation had been as a prostitute in the Syrian bawdy house.

'But meanwhile,' Simon continued, after spitting out a mouthful of the lukewarm water when he glimpsed a band of pilgrims in white cloaks emerging from the shade of the houses, men in whom he recognized Peter and his disciples armed with shepherd's staffs. 'But meanwhile – beneath the murky shroud of the heavens, within the dark walls of the earth, and in the dungeon of existence – despise wealth, as they teach you, deny the pleasures of the flesh, and scorn woman, that cup of nectar, that urn of bliss, in the name of their false paradise and out of fear of their false hell, as if this life were not hell. . .'

'Some choose the earthly kingdom, others the kingdom of heaven,' said Peter, leaning on his staff with both hands.

'Only he who has known wealth may despise it,' said Simon, squinting his larger eye at Peter. 'Only he who has known poverty may admire it. Only he who has experienced the pleasures of the flesh may deny them.'

'The Son of God experienced suffering,' said Peter.

'His miracles are proof of His righteousness,' one of Peter's disciples interjected.

'Miracles are no proof of righteousness,' Simon responded. 'Miracles serve as proof only for the gullible, the multitude. They are nothing but a craze introduced by your miserable Jew, the one who ended on the cross.'

'Only he who has the power to perform miracles may speak as you do,' Peter objected.

Then Simon jumped down from the wobbly barrel and landed eye-to-eye with his challenger. 'I will now fly up to the sky,' he said.

'I should like to see it,' Peter replied, with a quiver in his voice.

'I know the extent of my power,' said Simon, 'and I know I cannot reach the seventh heaven. But I shall go through six. Only thought can reach the seventh, because the seventh heaven is all light and bliss. And bliss is denied mortal man.'

'Enough philosophizing,' said one of Peter's disciples. 'If

you reach even that cloud up there, we shall respect you as we do the Nazarene.'

Hearing that there were some unusual doings afoot just outside the village, near the large olive tree, and that the chatter-box was at last about to do one of his fakir's tricks, a crowd gathered round again.

'Don't be gone too long,' one of the spectators called out mockingly. 'In fact, why not leave something behind as security?'

Simon unwound the flaxen rope from his waist and placed it at his feet. 'It is all I have.'

And Sophia said, 'Take this scarf. It's cold up there, as cold as at the bottom of a well.' And she put the scarf around his neck.

'These preparations are taking too long,' said Peter.

'He is waiting for the sun to go down,' added one of Peter's disciples, 'so he can run for it under cover of night.'

'Goodbye,' said Simon, kissing Sophia on the forehead.

'Farewell,' said one of Peter's disciples. 'Watch out you don't catch cold!'

Suddenly Simon jumped with both legs, like a cockerel, flapping his arms clumsily, and dust spread around his sandals.

'Cock-a-doodle-doo!' a joker cried, a smooth-cheeked young man with shrewd eyes that turned to slanting slits when he laughed.

Simon glanced over in his direction and said, 'It's not so easy, my boy! The earth exerts a hold on all bodies, on the merest feather, to say nothing of a human wreck of more than a hundredweight.'

Peter was unable to stifle his laughter at Simon's sophistry, and had to hide it in his beard.

'If you were as good at flying as you are at philosophy,' said the joker, 'you'd be soaring through the clouds by now.'

'Philosophizing is easier than flying, I admit,' said Simon, with sorrow in his voice. 'Even you know how to chatter, though never once in your miserable life have you wrenched yourself so much as a foot off the ground... And now let me collect my strength and my thoughts and concentrate with everything I have on the horror of our earthly existence, on the imperfection of the world, on the myriad lives torn asunder, on the beasts that devour one another, on the snake that bites a stag as it grazes in the shade, on the wolves that slaughter sheep, on the mantises that consume their males, on the bees that die after they sting, on the mothers who labor to bring us into the world, on the blind kittens children toss into rivers, on the terror of the fish in the whale's entrails and the terror of the beaching whale, on the sadness of an elephant dying of old age, on the butterfly's fleeting joy, on the deceptive beauty of the flower, on the fleeting illusion of a lovers' embrace, on the horror of spilt seed, on the impotence of the aging tiger, on the rotting of teeth in the mouth, on the myriad dead leaves lining the forest floor, on the fear of the fledgling when its mother pushes it out of the nest, on the infernal torture of the worm baking in the sun as if roasting in living fire, on the anguish of a lovers' parting, on the horror known by lepers, on the hideous metamorphoses of women's breasts, on wounds, on the pain of the blind...'

And all at once they saw the mortal body of Simon Magus detach itself from the ground, rise straight up, higher and higher, arms beating like fish gills, subtly, almost imperceptibly, hair and beard streaming in gentle flight, floating.

Not a cry, not a breath could be heard in the silence that suddenly settled upon the crowd. They stood stock-still, as if dumbfounded, their gaze fixed on the sky. Even the blind rolled their vacant, milky eyes upwards, for they, too, had grasped what the sudden silence meant, where the crowd had directed its attention, where all heads were turned.

Peter stood petrified too, his mouth open in amazement. He did not believe in miracles other than miracles of faith, and miracles could come from Him alone, the sole Miracle Worker, the One who had turned water into wine; all others were merely magic tricks, a matter of concealed ropes. Miracles were granted only to Christians, and among Christians only to those whose faith was as solid as a rock, like His.

Shaken for a moment, frightened by the illusion – for it could be nothing more than a sensory illusion, a case of Egyptian fairground sorcery – he rubbed his eyes, then looked over at the spot where Simon, called the Magus, had been standing (and therefore ought still to be standing). But he was not there, only his flaxen rope all coiled up like a snake, and the dust, now slowly settling, that Simon had stirred up as he hopped up and down like a clumsy rooster, flapping his arms like clipped wings. Then he raised his eyes to where the crowd's heads pointed, and again he saw the Magus. His silhouette stood out clearly against the white cloud. It looked like a gigantic eagle, but it was not an eagle; it was a man: the human arms, human legs, human head were still easily discernible, though, to tell the truth, whether the man approaching the cloud was actually Simon Magus was impossible to ascertain, because the facial features were beyond recognition.

Peter looked up at the white cloud and blinked to banish the illusion that had duped the entire crowd. For if the black silhouette approaching the cloud was in fact Simon, then His miracles and the truth of the Christian faith were *but one of the truths of this world* and not the sole truth, then the world was a mystery and faith an illusion, then his life had lost its foundation, then man was a mystery among mysteries, then the unity of the world and Creation was an unknown.

What must be – if he could believe his eyes – the mortal body of Simon Magus had now reached the cloud, a black speck that vanished for a moment, then stood out clearly against the low cloud's base, and finally disappeared for good in the white mist.

The silence lasted only a moment before it was broken by a sigh of wonder in the crowd; people fell on their knees, prostrated themselves, and rolled their heads as if in a trance. Even some of Peter's disciples bowed before the new pagan miracle they had just witnessed.

Then Peter closed his eyes and said, in Hebrew (because it is the natural language of saints, and lest the crowd should understand him), the following prayer: 'Our One and Only Father, who art in heaven, come to the aid of my senses, which have been deceived by a mirage; grant unto mine eyes keenness of sight and unto my mind the wisdom to avoid dreams and illusions and remain steadfast in Thy faith and in my love for Thy Son, Our Saviour. Amen.'

And God said unto him, 'Follow my counsel, O faithful servant. Say unto the people that the power of faith is greater than the snares of the senses; say it loudly, so that all may hear. And say unto them, loud, so that all may hear: God is one and His name is Elohim, and the Son of God is one and His name is Jesus, and faith is one and it is the Christian faith. And he who has just now soared up to the sky, Simon, called the Magus, is an apostate and a desecrator of God's teachings; he has indeed taken flight by dint of his will and his thoughts and is now flying, invisible, to the stars, borne by doubt and human curiosity, which, however, have their limits. And say unto them, loud, so that all may hear, that I was the One who granted him the power of temptation, that all his might and strength came from me, for it was I who suffered him to tempt Christian souls with his miracles, that I might show them there is no miracle without me, no power but mine. Speak thus unto them and have no fear.'

Then Peter opened his eyes, climbed up a mound of dried manure swarming with flies, and began to shout at the top of his voice, 'Listen, people, and hear!'

No one paid any attention to him. The people lay with their heads in the dust, as sheep lie in the shade of a grove on a hot day.

Again Peter shouted at the top of his voice, 'Listen, O people of Samaria, listen to what I have to tell you.'

A few people lifted their heads, the blind first.

'You have seen what you have seen. You have been the victims of a sensory illusion. That conjurer, that fakir who received his training in Egypt. . .'

'He kept his word,' said Sophia.

'By the time I count to ten,' Peter went on, taking no notice of her, 'his body will crash to the earth he so despised, fall like a stone at your feet, never again to rise from the dust. . . For God the One and Only so desires. One. . .'

'He flew, didn't he?' said Sophia. 'He proved he was a magus.'

'Two. . .'

'Even if he falls, he is the victor,' said Sophia.

Peter kept his eyes shut while he counted, as if wishing to gain time.

And then he heard a shriek going up from the crowd, and he opened his eyes. At the very spot where Simon had disappeared, a black speck was emerging from the cloud and starting to grow. The body of Simon Magus came hurtling to the earth like a stone, spinning on its longitudinal and transversal axes. As it grew bigger and more visible, the arms and legs could be seen flailing, and the crowd started running in all directions, apparently out of fear that the body plunging headlong from the heavens would land on one of their number.

From then on, everything happened very quickly. Like a sack of moist sand when it lands on the drayman's cart or like a sheep dropped by an eagle in flight, the body of Simon Magus crashed to the ground.

The first to approach it was Sophia the prostitute, his faithful companion. All she wanted was to cover his eyes with the scarf she had given him, but forced to close her own eyes at the horrible spectacle, she was unable to do even that. He lay on the ground, his skull fractured, his limbs broken, his face mutilated and streaming with blood, his intestines protruding like the entrails of a slaughtered ox; on the ground lay a heap of crushed, shattered bones and mangled flesh, and his burnoose, his sandals, and her scarf were entangled with the flesh and bones in a revolting mangled mess.

The people who came up to look at the sight heard Sophia say in tones of malediction, 'This is yet further proof of the truth of *his* teaching. Man's life is a Fall, and a hell, and the world is in the hands of tyrants. Cursed be the greatest of all tyrants, Elohim.'

Then she made for the desert, wailing.

2

According to another version, Simon Magus did not direct his challenge at the seventh heaven, but at the earth, the greatest of all Illusions.

So Simon lay on his back, his hands behind his head, in the shade of a giant olive tree, staring up at the sky, at 'the horror of the heavens.' The prostitute sat at his side, 'with her legs spread wide like a pregnant cow,' as a Christian polemist notes (though we cannot be certain whether he is reporting his own observations or citing an eyewitness – or simply making it all up). The olive tree and its meager shade remain the only hard facts amid the multifarious evidence in the curious story of Simon's miracles. And so, chance willed it that Peter and his men should come upon him there. Doubtless provoked by Sophia's unworthy bearing, one of the disciples, his head turned away to shield him from temptation, asked Simon whether it was better to sow on earth and reap in heaven or to cast one's seed to the wind – a scholastic question requiring an unambiguous answer.

Simon propped himself up on one elbow and, rising no farther, answered him over his shoulder, saying: *'All earth is earth, and where one sows is all the same. True communion comes from the commingling of man and woman.'*

'Any man and any woman?' Peter asked, nearly turning around in amazement.

'Woman is the urn of bliss,' said Simon. 'And you, like all dimwits, you stop up your ears to keep them free of blasphemy; you avert your gaze or flee when you have no answer.'

There followed a long theological discussion of Elohim, punishment, repentance, abnegation, soul and body, and the meaning of life, all of which was interspersed with scholastic arguments and quotations in Hebrew, Greek, Coptic, and Latin.

'The soul is Alpha and Omega,' Peter concluded. 'What is good is what is pleasing to God.'

'Works are not good or bad in themselves,' said Simon. 'Morality is defined by men, not God.'

'Acts of charity are a guarantee of life everlasting,' said Peter. 'Miracles are proof for those who still doubt.'

'Can your God repair the damage done to a virgin?' asked Simon, glancing at his companion.

'He has spiritual power,' said Peter, visibly disconcerted by the question.

Sophia smiled an ambiguous smile.

'What I mean is, has he any physical power?' Simon went on.

'He has,' said Peter, without hesitation. 'He has cured lepers, he has. . .'

'. . .changed water into wine, et cetera, et cetera,' Simon interjected.

'Yes,' Peter continued. 'Miracles are his calling. . .'

'I thought carpentry was his calling,' said Simon.

'And charity,' said Peter.

Finally, incensed by Peter's obstinacy and constant references to His miracles, Simon said, 'I can work miracles like your Nazarene.'

'That's easily said,' Peter replied, with a quiver in his voice.

'He's picked up all kinds of tricks in the bazaars of Egypt,' said one of Peter's disciples. 'We must beware of deceit.'

'Your Nazarene – what was his name again? – he could have studied Egyptian magic, too,' said Simon.

'His miracles occurred more than once,' said Peter.

'Bury me in the earth, six cubits deep,' said Simon after brief deliberation. 'In three days I shall rise up like your . . .'

'Jesus,' said Peter. 'You know very well what His name is.'

'That's right. Him.'

One of the disciples ran off to a nearby village and returned with a group of laborers who had been building a well in the valley. They had spades, shovels, and axes slung over their shoulders. The whole village, everything that could move, came running after them. News that an Egyptian sorcerer had appeared and was going to work a miracle had spread rapidly.

'Six cubits deep,' Simon repeated.

The laborers set to work, and soon the sandy surface had been replaced by some rather coarse gravel, then by a layer of dry, reddish earth. The shovels kept turning up clay with traces of roots in it; earthworms, sliced in two by the sharp blades, wriggled and writhed in the sun as if roasting in living fire.

Sophia stood silently beside the pit, which grew deeper and deeper, while Simon – like a lord for whom a well is being dug or a foundation laid – issued orders to the men, measured off the length and breadth of the pit with careful steps, lowered his flaxen rope into its depths, and crumbled earth and sand between his fingers.

When the coffin was ready – it was made of roughly hewn boards of fragrant cypress held together by wooden studs – Sophia took off her scarf and placed it around Simon's neck. 'It's cold down there, as cold as at the bottom of a well,' she said.

Simon then abruptly left her side and took hold of the coffin and shook it, as if wishing to test its solidity. Then he stepped in nimbly and stretched out on the bottom.

The laborers approached and, when he gave the sign, pounded the large studs into place with their broad axes. Peter whispered something to one of his disciples. The disciple went up and, having tested the studs, nodded.

Peter raised a slightly trembling arm, and the laborers slid some ropes under the coffin and lowered it carefully into the hole. Sophia stood to the side, motionless. Soil began falling on the lid; it made a noise like the beat of a large drum moving swiftly into the distance. Soon, on the spot where the hole had been, near the big olive tree, a mound resembling a sand dune took shape.

Peter climbed the mound, lifted his arms heavenwards, and started mumbling a prayer. His eyes shut, his head slightly cocked, he gave the impression of a man straining to catch far-off voices.

By the end of the day, the wind had erased all trace of bare feet and sandals from the shifting sands.

Three days later – it was a Friday – they dug up the coffin. Many more people gathered for the disinterment than had for the interment: news of the magus, fakir, conjurer had spread far and wide. As judges to whom everyone gave priority, Sophia, Peter, and his disciples stood closest to the pit.

They were struck by a revolting stench, as if from hell. Then, through the dug earth, they saw the boards of the coffin, which had darkened, as if they were rusting. The workers knocked out the studs and raised the lid. The face of Simon Magus was a mass of leprous corruption, and his eye sockets had worms peering out of them. Only his yellowish teeth remained intact, grinning as if he were convulsed or laughing.

Sophia covered her eyes with her hands and screamed. Then she turned slowly toward Peter and said in a voice that made him tremble: 'This, too, is proof of *his* teaching. Man's life is decay and perdition, and the world is in the hands of tyrants. Cursed be the greatest of all tyrants, Elohim.'

The people made way for her as she passed through their silent ranks and made for the desert, wailing.

Her mortal body returned to the brothel, while her spirit moved on to a new Illusion.

Last Respects

It happened in 1923 or 1924. In Hamburg, I think. During a time of stock-market disasters and giddy devaluation: the daily wages of a dock laborer came to seventeen billion marks, and decent prostitutes charged three times as much for their services. (Sailors in the port of Hamburg carried 'change' in cardboard boxes, under their arms.)

In one of the small pink rooms not far from the port, a prostitute named Mariette had died suddenly of pneumonia. Bandura, a Ukrainian sailor and revolutionary, claimed she had 'gone up in flames of love.' He was incapable of associating her *divine* body with even the slightest banality, and pneumonia was a 'bourgeois disease.' 'She went up in flames, at the stake,' he said. Although nearly five years had passed since the event, Bandura's voice grew hoarse and muffled whenever he spoke of it, as if he were choking on a cough. It was not only the result of alcohol, though the truth of it was that by then he had become a ruin abandoned by his kind, a huge rusty ship run aground and rotting in the shallows.

'Don't worry,' Bandura wheezed. 'No whore on earth was ever mourned with more sincerity, no whore ever paid such last respects.'

Greenhouse flower beds and abandoned outlying gardens had been ravaged for Mariette's funeral; dogs barked all night; the hounds were called out, and Alsatians straining at the collar, that canine crown of thorns; links of heavy chains slid up taut steel wires, clanging like the chains of all history's slaves; and no one had the slightest inkling, not even the tired old gardeners in whose ailing bones lay a history of ailments as enormous as the history of the proletariat, that on that night a small, separate revolution had taken place: the sailors of the port of Hamburg stormed the villas of the wealthy; the proletarian children of Le Havre, Marseilles, Antwerp massacred the gladioluses under cover of night, slitting stems at the root with sharp sailor's knives and trampling minor flora, unworthy of the knife, with heavy, scruffy boots. Parks were 'savagely overrun'; nor was the Municipal Garden spared, nor the garden in front of Town Hall, 'a stone's throw from Police Headquarters.' 'So barbarous an act,' said the news-papers, 'could have been perpetrated only by spirits of anarchist bent and ruthless flower smugglers.'

Mariette's grave was covered with armfuls of roses, white and red, freshly cut pine branches, chrysanthemums and tuberoses, sky-blue hydrangeas, decadent art-nouveau irises, the flower of lust, hyacinths and expensive black tulips, the flower of night, waxen mortuary lilies, the flower of virginity and First Communion, violet lilacs reeking of decay, low-born rhododendrons, and monstrous gladioluses (which were in the majority), soft-white and soft-pink, saintly, angelic gladioluses with their intrinsic sword-and-rose mystique, all of them together a sign of putrid wealth, of the cool mansions of the wealthy, lethally lush gladioluses watered by the sweat of weary old gardeners, the rosettes of watering cans, the artificial rain of artesian wells, to shield from the elements the lushly morbid growth of barren flowers devoid of fragrance, even fish fragrance, despite their fantastically jointed, lobster-claw structure, despite the blossoms' waxen wrinkles and the stamens' mock tentacles and the mock spines of the finely honed buds: all that monstrous lushness was incapable of exuding a single atom of scent, not even so much as a wild violet's worth. The crown of these floral fireworks consisted of magnolia branches purloined from the Botanical Gardens, lush branches of leathery leaves, each branch tipped with a single large flower like a silk ribbon in the hair of the 'society girls' whom Comrade Bandura likened (with his typical taste for overstatement) to harbor whores. Only cemeteries were spared, because in his call to 'all sailors, all longshoremen, all those who loved her' Bandura had requested *fresh* flowers only, expressly forbidding – doubtless in a rush of quasi-mystical inspiration – the desecration of graves. I believe I can reconstruct, approximately at least, the flow of his thought: You can't cheat death; flowers, like humans, follow a clear dialectical path and biological cycle – from blossom to decay; proletarians have a right to the same last respects as respectable citizens; whores are the product of class differences; whores are (therefore) worthy of the same flowers as young ladies from good families. And so on.

The silent procession led by Bandura did not raise its flags, red and black, until it had reached the outlying, proletarian part of town; there they unfurled in the wind with an ominous flutter, fire-red, night-black, symbols resembling the language of flowers yet not without social overtones.

At the border between the graves of the rich and the graves of the poor, Bandura stumbled his way up a high podium of black marble slabs (a bronze angel held a wreath over a long-dead girl) and, before the quiet, bareheaded crowd of sailors and heavily made-up prostitutes, delivered his funeral oration. He began with a short, schematic account of her life: the painful existence of a child from a proletarian family with a laundress for a mother and a scoundrel for a father, who ended his days a drunken stevedore in the port of Marseilles. And while the sailor and revolutionary Bandura tried, with tight

throat and cracked voice, to reduce his eulogy – that sad sum-
mation of a wretched life – to a chronicle of social injustice
and class struggle, declaiming words of hate as if reciting
Bakunin, he could not help reviewing the living pictures of
that life as they passed before him like photographs in an old
album (and I am certain they mingled imperceptibly with
memories of his own childhood): a basement in morbid
semi-darkness, cigarette smoke, and the reek of wine and an-
isette; harrowing scenes of family quarrels, fights, screaming
and sobbing; bedbugs burning, popping under a torch of
lighted newsprint, the flame licking the already sooty grooves
and joints of iron army beds; the evening's delousing by
flickering lamplight, the children leaning over one another's
heads monkey-like and discovering clusters of the pests at the
roots of black and blond tufts; a mother's hands, swollen like
boiled goatfish from taking in washing. . .

His speech over the open grave was interrupted only by
occasional hysterical sobs from the old whores (no one perhaps showed more painfully the transience of the flesh and the
impending disaster of decay) and hoarse coughs and sniffles
from the longshoremen, though he had no way of knowing
whether it was actually coughing or a tough, sailor's brand of
crying, a male surrogate for crying, the same substitute for
sighs and tears he himself was using as he gave the speech.
(Listening to his voice – like the voice of a stranger or a
scratchy phonograph – he mentally leafed through the old
picture album in chronological order, from his original
encounter with Mariette.)

He first laid eyes on her one evening in 1919, in the port of
Hamburg, where he had just gone ashore from the *Franken*. It
was a beautiful gray November evening with streetlamps
flickering in the mist. He had orders to make contact with the
apparat in a local dive the next day (a password had been

agreed) and until then he was to go unnoticed, to refrain from standing out in any way – in bearing, speech, behavior, or appearance – from the hundred, the thousand sailors who had gone ashore that day. He walked along 'Doll Street' mingling with the drunken sailors – and sober informers playing drunken sailors – and peered through the low windows into discreetly pink-lit rooms. The red-shaded wall lamp cast a light like that of the Flemish masters in portraits of Lady in a Violet Interior, while a screen painted over with decadent irises, the flower of debauchery, hid the mysteries of the Intimate (which attracts by concealment like folds and slits in a dress): the settee upholstered in brocade and solid as a ship – oh, Bandura knew the shape of things long before he came to know Mariette! – the sparkling white porcelain basin and shapely high-handled pitcher. The lamp's pink light glitters on the screen's glossy fabric, the irises recede into darkness, as does the red brocade on the chair, in the center of the window, where the Lady sits. She is turned toward the spectator in semi-profile, the rose-colored lamplight bending this way and that in the folds of her dress. Her legs are crossed, her hands occupied by knitting. The flicker of needles above the yarn. Long, blond hair falling over bared shoulders down to half-bared breasts. A second Lady, in the next window, holds a book. She is like a novice reading the Bible. From under the strawberry-blond hair that slightly veils her face a glint of light is reflected off her eyeglasses. (Moving a bit closer, the observer discovers the title, *The Count of Monte Cristo*, printed in large letters.) She is wearing a dark dress with a white lace collar, a camp follower who looks like a student at Heidelberg. . . And then he saw her, Mariette. She sat with her legs crossed like the others and her bottom sticking out, with a cigarette in her hand and the usual bright satin dress hugging her body, but there was something in her bearing, her appearance, the pale pink glow in which she was immersed as in an aquarium (the sailor's eternal Siren) that immediately attracted Bandura. Yet not until he had entered her room and she had drawn the heavy green velvet curtain across the window and placed her warm hand under his shirt, not until then did he realize: Mariette was not meant to play a role, be it Housewife or Knitter or Student or Novice; she was the only one who needed no complicated and carefully rehearsed choreography; she was unique, inimitable; she *was* a harbor whore.

'She loved and aided sailors from all ports,' Bandura roared out over the open grave as if at a rally, 'and she had no prejudices against skin color, race, or religion. She pressed her breasts – "small but beautiful," as Napoleon Bonaparte, the emperor of crime, used to say – with equal ardor to the black, sweaty chests of New York sailors, the yellow hairless chests of the Malaysians, the bear-like paws of Hamburg stevedores, and the tattoos of the Albert Canal pilots; her lily-white neck, like a seal of universal brotherhood, had been crushed by Maltese crosses, crucifixes, Stars of David, Russian icons, shark's teeth, and mandrake talismans, and between her tender thighs flowed a river of hot sperm that merged in her warm vagina as in the home port of all sailors, the mouth of all rivers. . .'

Bandura listened to his own voice, remote and cold, and images from Mariette's life kept coming to him but without any clear chronology, like the wind riffling through the leaves of an album, and as if he himself, Bandura, had seen everything there with his own eyes. (After love, in the proximity of a man she *really* loved – and this tender-hearted revolutionary was one of them – Mariette could talk about herself as if she were at confession. She would reminisce with a curious kind of nostalgia, as if all the brutal stories, full of loathsome detail, were unimportant in and of themselves, the only thing of importance being that it had all happened long ago, she had been *young* then, *presque une enfant*, almost a child.) And he saw some disgusting little Greek take her by the hand one Carnival evening, pale and slightly drunk from skimming the foam off beers like a child; saw her tag after the Greek with the tiny steps of a hungry, obedient animal through the narrow streets of Marseilles and down to the port; saw her start up the steps of a dark tenement in the vicinity of the harbor warehouses, pulling herself along by a makeshift railing of thick cordage; then followed her, with the same vague fury, as she made her confident way toward the third-story door (the Greek still standing at the foot of the stairs, in case she changed her mind). Then the scene switched back to the streets of Marseilles, where a heavily made-up Mariette stood leaning against a stone wall, supporting herself on one leg like an injured bird. . .

'All of us here, Comrades,' Bandura went on, 'we are all members of one large family, lovers, fiancés – I mean, husbands of the same wife, knights of the same lady, cousins-in-cunt, who have swilled at the same source, swigged rum from the same bottle, wept drunken tears on the same shoulder, and heaved into the same basin, the one over there, behind the green screen. . .'

When Bandura's cracked voice fell silent, the first lumps of earth – cast by the rough hands of sailors and stevedores, who crumbled them as if salting the innards of a gigantic fish – began to beat against the coffin. From somewhere above the grave came the sound of fluttering silk, red and black flags turned to mere funeral trappings. Then earth began to rain down on the grave by the shovelful, drumming dully on the coffin with the sound an ear hears when pressed against the frantic heart of a bawd after love. They tossed the flowers in singly, then in bunches, and eventually by the armful, passing them along from one to the next, hand to hand, a collective harvest, all the

way from the chapel to the paupers' section, where crosses suddenly shrink and granite tombs and bronze monuments give
way to stone markers and rotting wood. And no one will ever
know what made them do it, what impulse, what drunken
whim, what pain – class hatred or Jamaica rum? – made them
violate Bandura's order, but all at once a miracle of revolutionary disobedience took place, an elemental, irrational uprising:
sailors and streetwalkers, a hard-boiled lot, suddenly took to
raving and exaltation, tears and teeth-gnashing as they tore out
the noble gladioluses, bloodied their hands on rose stems,
pulled up tulips with their bulbs, bit off carnations, passing
them along from one to the next, hand to hand, and by the armful. Up grew a mountain of flowers and greenery, a stake of
tulips, hydrangeas, and roses, a charnel house of gladioluses, the
cross above the fresh burial mound and the burial mound itself
disappearing under the enormous stack of flowers with the
slightly rank aroma of lilacs past their prime.

By the time the police intervened, the finer sections of the
cemetery had been stripped bare, devastated, as if, according
to press reports, 'a swarm of locusts had passed through the
gloomy precinct.' (*Rote Fahne* carried an unsigned article con-
demning police brutality and the arrest and deportation of
some twenty sailors.)

'Take off your cap,' says Bandura to the man he has been
talking to. In a sudden surge of pain Johann or Jan Valtin (I
think that's what his name was) tries to recall Mariette's face.
All he can come up with is a tiny body and a hoarse laugh.
Then, for a moment, he catches a mental glimpse of her smile,
a shadow of her face, but soon they too dissolve.

'*Don't worry,*' says Bandura. '*No young lady from a good
family was ever mourned with more sincerity, no lady was ever
paid such last respects.*'

The Encyclopedia of the Dead
(A Whole Life)

For M.

Last year, as you know, I went to Sweden at the invitation of the Institute for Theater Research. A Mrs Johansson, Kristina Johansson, served as my guide and mentor. I saw five or six productions, among which a successful *Godot* – for prisoners – was most worthy of note. Ten days later, when I had returned home, I was still living in that far-off world as if in a dream.

Mrs Johansson was a determined woman, and she intended to use those ten days to show me everything there was to see in Sweden, everything that might interest me 'as a woman.' She even included the famous *Vasa*, the sailing ship that had been hauled out of the sludge after several hundred years, preserved like a pharaoh's mummy. One evening, after a performance of *Ghost Sonata* at the Dramaten, my hostess took me to the Royal Library. I barely had time to eat a sandwich in a bar.

It was about eleven by then, and the building was closed. But Mrs Johansson showed a pass to the man at the door, and he let us in, muttering. He held a large ring of keys in his hand, like the guard who had let us into the Central Prison the day before to see *Godot*. My hostess, having delivered me into the hands of this Cerberus, said she would call for me in the morning at the hotel; she told me to examine the library in God's peace, the gentleman would call me a cab, he was at my disposal. . . What could I do but accept her kind offer? The guard escorted me to an enormous door, which he unlocked, and then switched on a dim light and left me alone. I heard the key turn in the lock behind me; there I was, in a library like a dungeon.

A draft blew in from somewhere, rippling the cobwebs, which, like dirty scraps of gauze, hung from the bookshelves as over select bottles of old wine in a cellar. All the rooms were alike, connected by a narrow passageway, and the draft, whose source I could not identify, penetrated everywhere.

It was at that point, even before I had had a good look at the books (and just after noticing the letter *C* on one of the volumes in the third room), that I caught on: each room housed one letter of the alphabet. This was the third. And, indeed, in the next section all the books were marked with the letter *D*. Suddenly, driven by some vague premonition, I broke into a run. I heard my steps reverberating, a multiple echo that faded away in the darkness. Agitated and out of breath, I arrived at the letter *M* and *with a perfectly clear goal in mind* opened one of the books. I had realized – perhaps I had read about it somewhere – that this was the celebrated *Encyclopedia of the Dead*. Everything had come clear in a flash, even before I opened the massive tome.

The first thing I saw was his picture, the only illustration, set into the double-column text in roughly the middle of the page. It was the photograph you saw on my desk. It was taken in 1936, on November 12, in Maribor, just after his discharge from the army. Under the picture were his name and, in parentheses, the years 1910–79.

You know that my father died recently and that I had been very close to him from my earliest years. But I don't want to talk about that here. What concerns me now is that he died less than two months before my trip to Sweden. One of the main reasons I decided to take the trip was to escape my grief. I thought, as people in adversity are wont to think, that a change of scene would help me escape the pain, as if we did not bear our grief *within* ourselves.

Cradling the book in my arms and leaning against the rickety wooden shelves, I read his biography completely oblivious of time. As in medieval libraries, the books were fastened by thick chains to iron rings on the shelves. I did not realize this until I tried to move the heavy volume closer to the light.

I was suddenly overcome with anguish; I felt I had overstayed my welcome and Mr Cerberus (as I called him) might come and ask me to halt my reading. I therefore started skimming through the paragraphs, turning the open book, insofar as the chain would allow, in the direction of the pale light shed by the lamp. The thick layer of dust that had gathered along their edges and the dangling scraps of cobwebs bore clear witness to the fact that no one had handled the volumes in a long time. They were fettered to one another like galley slaves, but their chains had no locks.

So this is the famous *Encyclopedia of the Dead*, I thought to myself. I had pictured it as an ancient book, a 'venerable' book, something like the Tibetan Book of the Dead or the Cabala or the *Lives of the Saints* – one of those esoteric creations of the human spirit that only hermits, rabbis, and monks can enjoy. When I saw that I might go on reading until dawn and be left without any concrete trace of what I had read for myself or my mother, I decided to copy out several of the most important passages and make a kind of summary of my father's life.

The facts I have recorded here, in this notebook, are ordinary, encyclopedia facts, unimportant to anyone but my mother and me: names, places, dates. They were all I managed to jot down, in haste, towards dawn. What makes the *Encyclopedia* unique (apart from its being the only existing copy) is the way it depicts human relationships, encounters, landscapes – the multitude of details that make up a human life. The reference (for example) to my father's place of birth is not only complete and accurate ('Kraljevčani, Glina township, Sisak district, Banija province') but is accompanied by both geographical and historical details. Because *it* records everything. Everything. The countryside of his native region is rendered so vividly that as I read, or rather flew over the lines and paragraphs, I felt I was in the heart of it: the snow on distant mountain peaks, the bare trees, the frozen river with children skating past as in a Brueghel landscape. And among those children I saw him clearly, my father, although he was not yet my father, only he who would become my father, who *had been* my father. Then the countryside suddenly turned green and buds blossomed on the trees, pink and white, hawthorn bushes flowered before my eyes, the sun arched over the village of Kraljevčani, the village church bells chimed, cows mooed in their barns, and the scarlet reflection of the morning sun glistened on the cottage windows and melted the icicles hanging from the gutters.

Then, as if it were all unfolding before my eyes, I saw a funeral procession headed in the direction of the village cemetery. Four men, hatless, were carrying a fir casket on their shoulders, and at the head of the procession walked a man, hat in hand, whom I knew to be – for that is what the book said – my paternal grandfather Marko, the husband of the deceased, whom they were laying to rest. The book tells everything about her as well: date of birth, cause of illness and death, progression of disease. It also indicates what garments she was buried in, who bathed her, who placed the coins on her eyes, who bound her chin, who carved the casket, where the timber was felled. That may give you an idea – some idea, at least – of the copiousness of the information included in *The*

Encyclopedia of the Dead by those who undertake the difficult and praiseworthy task of recording – in what is doubtless an objective and impartial manner – everything that can be recorded concerning those who have completed their earthly journey and set off on the eternal one. (For they believe in the miracle of biblical resurrection, and they compile their vast catalogue in preparation for that moment. So that everyone will be able to find not only his fellow men but also – and more important – his own forgotten past. When the time comes, this compendium will serve as a great treasury of memories and a unique proof of resurrection.) Clearly, they make no distinction, where a life is concerned, between a provincial merchant and his wife, between a village priest (which is what my great-grandfather was) and a village bell ringer called Ćuk, whose name also figures in the book. The only condition – something I grasped at once, it seems to have come to me even before I could confirm it – for inclusion in *The Encyclopedia of the Dead* is that no one whose name is recorded here may appear in any other encyclopedia. I was struck from the first, as I leafed through the book – one of the thousands of *M* volumes – by the absence of famous people. (I received immediate confirmation as I turned the pages with frozen fingers, looking for my father's name.) The *Encyclopedia* did not include separate listings for Mažuranić or Meyerhold or Malmberg or Maretić, who wrote the grammar my father used in school, or Meštrović, whom my father had once seen in the street, or Dragoslav Maksimović, a lathe operator and Socialist deputy whom my grandfather had known, or Tasa Milojević, Kautsky's translator, with whom my father had once conversed at the 'Russian Tsar' café. It is the work of a religious organization or sect whose democratic program stresses an egalitarian vision of the world of the dead, a vision that is doubtless inspired by some biblical precept and aims at redressing human injustices and granting all God's creatures an equal place in eternity. I was also quick to grasp that the *Encyclopedia* did not delve into the dark distance of history and time, that it came into being shortly after 1789. The odd caste of erudites must have members all over the world digging tirelessly and discreetly through obituaries and biographies, processing their data, and delivering them to headquarters in Stockholm. (I wondered for a moment whether Mrs Johansson might not be one of them. Had she brought me to the Library deliberately, after I confided my grief to her, so that I would discover *The Encyclopedia of the Dead* and find a grain of comfort in it?) That is all I can surmise, all I infer about their work. The reason for their secrecy resides, I believe, in the Church's long history of persecution, though work on an encyclopedia such as this understandably requires a certain discretion if the pressures of human vanity are to be avoided and attempts at corruption thwarted.

No less amazing than their secret activities, however, was their style, an unlikely amalgam of encyclopedic conciseness and biblical eloquence. Take, for example, the meager bit of information I was able to get down in my notebook: *there* it is condensed into a few lines of such intensity that suddenly, as if by magic, the reader's spirit is overwhelmed by the radiant landscape and swift succession of images. We find a three-year-old boy being carried up a mountain path to see his maternal grandfather on a sweltering sunny day, while in the background – the second or third plane, if that is what it is called – there are soldiers, revenue officers, and police, distant cannon thunder and muffled barking. We find a pithy chronology of the First World War: trains clanking past a market town, a brass band playing, water gurgling in the neck of a canteen, glass shattering, kerchiefs fluttering. . . Each item has its own paragraph, each period its own poetic essence and metaphor – not always in chronological order but in a strange symbiosis of past, present, and future. How else can we explain the plaintive comment in the text – the 'picture album' covering his first five years, which he spent with his grandfather in Komogovina – the comment that goes, if I remember correctly, 'Those *would be* the finest years of his life'? Then come condensed images of childhood, reduced, so to speak, to ideographs: names of teachers and friends, the boy's 'finest years' against a backdrop of changing seasons, rain splashing off a happy face, swims in the river, a toboggan speeding down a snow-swept hill, trout fishing, and then – or, if possible, simultaneously – soldiers returning from the battlefields of Europe, a canteen in the boy's hands, a shattered gas mask abandoned on an embankment. And names, life stories. The widower Marko meeting his future wife, Sofija Rebrača, a native of Komogovina, the wedding celebration, the toasts, the village horse race, pennants and ribbons flapping, the exchange-of-rings ceremony, singing and kolo-dancing outside the church doors, the boy dressed up in a white shirt, a sprig of rosemary in his lapel.

Here, in my notebook, I have recorded only the word 'Kraljevčani,' but the *Encyclopedia* devotes several dense paragraphs to this period, complete with names and dates. It describes how he awoke on that day, how the cuckoo in the clock on the wall roused him from his fitful sleep. It contains the names of the coachmen, the names of the neighbors who made up the escort, a portrait of the schoolmaster, the guidance he offered to the boy's new mother, the priest's counsels, the words of those who stood at the outskirts of the village to wave them one last farewell.

Nothing, as I have said, is lacking, nothing omitted, neither the condition of the road nor the hues of the sky, and the list of paterfamilias Marko's worldly possessions is complete to the last detail. Nothing has been forgotten, not even the names of the authors of old textbooks and primers full of well-meaning advice, cautionary tales, and biblical parables. Every period of life, every experience is recorded: every fish caught, every page read, the name of every plant the boy ever picked.

And here is my father as a young man, his first hat, his first carriage ride, at dawn. Here are the names of girls, the words of the songs sung at the time, the text of a love letter, the newspapers read – his entire youth compressed into a single paragraph.

Now we are in Ruma, where my father received his secondary-school education. Perhaps this example will give you an idea of how pansophical, to use an old word, *The Encyclopedia of the Dead* actually is. The principle is clear, yet the erudition, the need to record it all, everything a human life is made of, are enough to take one's breath away. What we have here is a brief history of Ruma, a meteorological map, a description of the railway junction; the name of the printer and everything printed at the time – every newspaper, every book; the plays put on by touring companies and the attractions of touring circuses; a description of a brickyard. . . where a young man, leaning against an acacia, is whispering a mixture of romantic and rather ribald words into a girl's ear (we have the complete text). And everything – the train, the printing press, *The Bumptious Bumpkin*, the circus elephant, the track forking off in the direction of Šabac – it all figures here only insofar as it pertains to the individual in question. There are also excerpts from school reports: grades, drawings, names of classmates, until the next-to-the-last year (section B), when the young man had words with Professor L.D., the history and geography teacher.

Suddenly we are in the heart of a new city. It is 1928; the young man is wearing a cap with a final-year insignia on it and has grown a mustache. (He will wear it for the rest of his life. Once, fairly recently, his razor slipped and he shaved it off completely. When I saw him, I burst into tears: he was some-body else. In my tears there was a vague, fleeting realization of how much I would miss him when he died.) Now here he is in front of the Café Central, then at a cinema, where a piano plays while *A Trip to the Moon* unfolds on the screen. Later we find him looking over newly posted announcements on the notice board in Jelačić Square, one of which – and I mention it only as a curiosity – announces a lecture by Krleža. The name of Anna Eremija – a maternal aunt, in whose Jurišić Street flat in Zagreb he will later live – figures here side by side with the names of Križaj, the opera singer, whom he once passed in the Upper Town; Ivan Labus, the cobbler who repaired his shoes; and a certain Ante Dutina, in whose bakery he bought his rolls . . .

In that distant year of 1929, one approached Belgrade via the Sava Bridge, probably with the same joy of arrival as one feels today. The train wheels clatter as they pass over the metal trestles, the Sava flows mud-green, a locomotive blows its whistle and loses speed, and my father appears at a second-class window, peering out at the distant view of an unfamiliar city. The morning is fresh, the fog slowly lifts off the horizon, black smoke puffs from the funnel of the steamer *Smederevo*, a muf-fled horn hoots its imminent departure for Novi Sad.

With brief interruptions, my father spent approximately fifty years in Belgrade, and the sum of his experiences – the total of some eighteen thousand days and nights (432,000 hours) is covered here, in this book of the dead, in a mere five or six pages! And yet, at least in broad outline, chronology is respected: the days flow like the river of time, toward the mouth, toward death.

In September of that year, 1929, my father enrolled in a school that taught surveying, and the *Encyclopedia* chronicles the creation of the Belgrade School of Surveying and gives the text of the inaugural lecture by its director, Professor Stojković (who enjoined the future surveyors to serve king and country loyally, for on their shoulders lay the heavy burden of mapping the new borders of our homeland). The names of the glorious campaigns and no less glorious defeats of the First World War – Kajmakčalan, Mojkovac, Cer, Kolubara, Drina – alternate with the names of professors and students who fell in battle, with my father's grades in trigonometry, draftsmanship, history, religion, and calligraphy. We find also the name Rosa, Roksanda, a flower girl with whom D.M. 'trifled,' as they said in those days, along with the names of Borivoj-Bora Ilić, who ran a café; Milenko Azanja, a tailor; Kosta Stavroski, at whose place he stopped every morning for a hot *burek*; and a man named Krtinić, who fleeced him once at cards. Next comes a list of films and soccer matches he saw, the dates of his excursions to Avala and Kosmaj, the weddings and funerals he attended, the names of the streets where he lived (Cetinjska, Empress Milica, Gavrilo Princip, King Peter I, Prince Miloš, Požeška, Kamenička, Kosmajska, Brankova), the names of the authors of his geography, geometry, and planimetry texts, titles of the books he enjoyed (*King of the Mountain, Stanko the Bandit, The Peasant Revolt*), church services, circus performances, gymnastics demonstrations, school functions, art exhibits (where a watercolor by my father was commended by the jury). We also find mention of the day he smoked his first cigarette, in the school lavatory, under the influence of one Ivan Gerasimov, the son of a Russian émigré, who took him one week later to a then-celebrated Belgrade café, with a Gypsy orchestra and Russian counts and officers weeping to guitars and balalaikas... Nothing is omitted: the ceremonial unveiling of the Kalemegdan monument, food poisoning from ice cream bought on the corner of Macedonia Street, the shiny pointed shoes purchased with the money his father gave him for passing his examinations.

The next paragraph tells of his departure for Užička Požega in 1933, in May. Traveling with him on the train, second class, is the unfortunate Gerasimov, the émigré's son. It is their first assignment: they are to survey the terrain of Serbia, make cadastral and cartographic sketches. They take turns carrying the leveling rod and the theodolite; protecting their heads with straw hats – it is summer by now, and the sun is beating down – they climb hills, call, shout back and forth to each other; the autumn rains begin; pigs start grubbing, the cattle start getting restless; the theodolite has to be kept sheltered: it attracts lightning. In the evenings they drink slivovitz with Milenković, the village schoolmaster, the spit turns, Gerasimov curses first in Russian, then in Serbian, the brandy is strong. Poor Gerasimov will die of pneumonia in November of that year, with D.M. standing over his deathbed, listening to his delirious ramblings – just as he will stand over his grave, head bowed, hat in hand, meditating on the transitory nature of human existence.

That is what remains in my memory; that is what remains in the notes I hurriedly jotted down with my frozen fingers on that night or, rather, morning. And it represents two entire years, two seemingly monotonous years, when from May to November – bandit season – D.M. drags the tripod and the theodolite up hill and down dale, the seasons revolve, the rivers overflow their banks and return to them, the leaves turned first green, then yellow, and my father sits in the shade of blossoming plum trees, then takes refuge under the eaves of a house as flashes of lightning illuminate the evening landscape and thunder reverberates through the ravines.

It is summer, the sun is blazing, and our surveyors (he has a new partner named Dragović) stop at a house (street and number noted) at noon, knock on the door, ask for water. A girl comes out and gives them a pitcher of ice-cold water, as in a folk tale. That girl – as you may have guessed – will become my mother.

I won't try to recount it all from memory, everything, the way it is recorded and depicted *there* – the date and manner of the betrothal, the traditional wedding where money is no object, the range of picturesque folkways that were part of that life: it would all seem insufficient, fragmentary, compared with *the original*. Still, I can't help mentioning that the text gives a list of the witnesses and guests, the name of the priest who officiated, the toasts and songs, the gifts and givers, the food and drink. Next, chronologically, comes a period of five months, between November and May, when the newlyweds settled in Belgrade; the *Encyclopedia* includes the floor plan and furniture arrangement, the price of the stove, bed, and wardrobe, as well as certain intimate details that in such instances are always so alike and always so different. After all – and this is what I consider the compilers' central message – nothing in the history of mankind is ever repeated, things that at first glance seem the same are scarcely even similar; each individual is a star unto himself, everything happens always and never, all things repeat themselves endlessly and unrepeatably. (This is why the authors of the majestic monument to diversity that is *The Encyclopedia of the Dead* insist on individuality; this is why every human being is sacred to them.)

Were it not for the compilers' obsession with the idea of the uniqueness of every human being and the singularity of every event, what would be the point of providing the names of the priest and the registrar, a description of the wedding dress, or the name of Gledić, a village outside Kraljevo, along with all those details that connect man and place? For now we come to my father's arrival 'in the field,' his stay from May to November – bandit season again – in various villages. We find the name of Jovan Radojković (at whose inn, in the evenings, the surveyors drink chilled wine on credit) and of a child, Svetozar, who became my father's godson at the request of a certain Stevan Janjić, and of a Dr Levstik, a Slovene exile, who prescribed medication for my father's gastritis, and of a girl named Radmila-Rada Mavreva, with whom he had a roll in the hay in a stable somewhere.

As for my father's military service, the book traces the marches he took with the Fifth Infantry stationed in Maribor, and specifies the names and ranks of the officers and N.C.O.s and the names of the men in his barracks, the quality of the food in the mess, a knee injury sustained on a night march, a reprimand received for losing a glove, the name of the café at which he celebrated his transfer to Požarevac.

At first glance it may seem quite the same as any military service, any transfer, but from the standpoint of the *Encyclopedia* both Požarevac and my father's seven months in the barracks there were unique: never again, *never*, would a certain D.M., surveyor, in the autumn of 1935, draw maps near the stove of the Požarevac barracks and think of how, two or three months before, on a night march, he had caught a glimpse of the sea.

The sea he glimpsed for the first time at twenty-five, from the slopes of Velebit mountain on April 28, 1935, would remain within him – a revelation, a dream sustained for some forty years with undiminished intensity, a secret, a vision never put into words. After all those years he was not quite sure himself whether what he had seen was the open sea or merely the horizon, and the only true sea for him remained the aquamarine of maps, where depths are designated by a darker shade of blue, shallows by a lighter shade.

That, I think, was why for years he refused to go away on holiday, even at a time when union organizations and tourist agencies sent people flocking to seaside resorts. His opposition betrayed an odd anxiety, a fear of being disillusioned, as if a close encounter with the sea might destroy the distant vision that had dazzled him on April 28, 1935, when for the first time in his life he glimpsed, from afar, at daybreak, the glorious blue of the Adriatic.

All the excuses he invented to postpone that encounter with the sea were somehow unconvincing: he didn't want to spend his summers like a vulgar tourist, he couldn't spare the money (which was not far from the truth), he had a low tolerance for the sun (though he had spent his life in the most blistering heat), and would we please leave him in peace, he did very well in Belgrade behind closed blinds. His romance with the sea is elaborated in this chapter of *The Encyclopedia of the Dead* in great detail, from that first lyrical sighting, in 1935, to the actual encounter, face to face, some forty years later.

It took place – his first true encounter with the sea – in 1975, when at last, after pestering by the whole family, he agreed to go to Rovinj with my mother and stay at the house of some friends who were away for the summer.

He came back early, dissatisfied with the climate, dissatisfied with the restaurant service, dissatisfied with the television programs, dissatisfied the crowds, the polluted water, the jellyfish, the prices and general 'highway robbery.' Of the sea itself, apart from complaints about pollution ('The tourists use it as a public toilet') and jellyfish ('They're attracted by human stench, like lice'), he said nothing, not a word. He dismissed it with a wave of the hand. Only now do I realize what he meant: his age-old dream of the Adriatic, that distant vision, was finer and keener, purer and stronger than the filthy water where fat men paddled about with oil-slathered women, 'black as pitch'.

That was the last time he went to the seaside for his summer holiday. Now I know that something died in him then, like a dear friend – a distant dream, a distant illusion (if it was an illusion) that he had borne within him for forty years.

As you can see, I've just made a forty-year leap forward in his biography, but chronologically speaking we are still back in 1937, 1938, by which time D.M. had two daughters, myself and my sister (the son was yet to come), conceived in the depths of the Serbian hinterland, villages like Petrovac-on-the-Mlava or Despotovac, Stepojevac, Bukovac, Ćuprija, Jelašica, Mateje-vica, Čečina, Vlasina, Knjaževac, or Podvis. Draw a map of the region in your mind, enlarging every one of the dots on the map or military chart (1:50,000) to their actual dimensions; mark the streets and houses he lived in; then walk into an courtyard, a house; sketch the layout of the rooms; prepare an inventory of the furniture and the orchard; and don't forget the names of the flowers growing in the garden behind the house or the news in the papers he reads, news of the Ribbentrop–Molotov Pact, of the flight of the Yugoslav royal government, of the prices of lard and coal, of the feats of the flying ace Aleksić. . . That is how the master encyclopedists go about it.

As I've said before, each event connected with his personal destiny, every bombardment of Belgrade, every advance of German troops to the east and their every retreat, is con-sidered from his point of view and in accordance with how it affects his life. There is mention of a Palmotićeva Street house, with all the essentials of the building and its inhabitants noted, because it was in the cellar of that house that he – and all of us – sat out the bombing of Belgrade; by the same token, there is a description of the country house in Stepojevac (name of owner, layout, etc., included) where Father sheltered us for the rest of the war, as well as the prices of bread, meat, lard, poultry, and brandy. You will find my father's talk with the Knjaževac chief of police and a document, dated 1942, relieving him of his duties, and if you read carefully you will see him gathering leaves in the Botanical Gardens or along Palmotićeva Street, pressing them and pasting them into his daughter's herbarium, writing out 'Dandelion (*Taraxacum officinale*)' or 'Linden (*Tilia*)' in the calligraphic hand he used when entering 'Adriatic Sea' or 'Vlasina' on maps.

The vast river of his life, this family novel, branches off into many tributaries, and side by side with the account of his stint in the sugar refinery in 1943–44 runs a kind of digest or chronicle of the fate of my mother and of us, his children – whole volumes condensed into a few cogent paragraphs. Thus, his early rising is linked to my mother's (she is off to one village or another to barter an old wall clock, part of her dowry, for a hen or a piece of bacon) and to our, the children's, departure for school. This morning ritual (the strains of 'Lilli Marlene' in the background come from a radio somewhere in the neighborhood) is meant to convey the family atmosphere in the sacked surveyor's home during the years of occupation (meager breakfasts of chicory and zwieback) and to give an idea of the 'fashions' of the time, when people wore earmuffs, wooden-soled shoes, and army-blanket overcoats.

The fact that, while working at the Milišić Refinery as a day laborer my father brought home molasses under his coat, at great risk, has the same significance for *The Encyclopedia of the Dead* as the raid on the eye clinic in our immediate vicinity or the exploits of my Uncle Cveja Karakašević, a native of Ruma, who filched what he could from the German officers' club at 7 French Street, where he worked as a 'supplier.' The curious circumstance, also Cveja Karakašević's doing, that several times during the German occupation we dined on fattened carp (which would spend the night in the large enamel tub in our bathroom) and washed it down with French champagne from the same officers' club, the '*Drei Husaren*', did not, of course, escape the attention of the *Encyclopedia*'s compilers. By the same token, and in keeping with the logic of their program (that there is nothing insignificant in a human life, no hierarchy of events), they entered all our childhood illnesses – mumps, tonsillitis, whooping cough, rashes – as well as a bout of lice and my father's lung trouble (their diagnosis tallies with Dr Djurović's: emphysema, due to heavy smoking). But you will also find a bulletin on the Bajlonova Marketplace notice board with a list of executed hostages that includes close friends and acquaintances of my father's; the names of patriots whose bodies swung from telegraph poles on Terazije, in the very center of Belgrade; the words of a German officer demanding to see his *Ausweis* at the station restaurant in Niš; the description of a Chetnik wedding in Vlasotinci, with rifles going off all through the night.

The Belgrade street battles in October 1944 are described from his point of view and from the perspective of Palmotićeva Street: the artillery rolling by, a dead horse lying on the corner. The deafening roar of the caterpillar treads momentarily drowns out the interrogation of a *Volksdeutscher* named Franjo Hermann, whose supplications pass easily through the thin wall of a neighboring building where an OZNA security officer metes out the people's justice and revenge. The burst of machine-gun fire in the courtyard next door reverberating harshly in the abrupt silence that follows the passing of a Soviet tank, a splash of blood on the wall that my father would see from the bathroom window, and the corpse of the unfortunate Hermann, in fetal position – they are all recorded in *The Encyclopedia of the Dead*, accompanied by the commentary of a hidden observer.

For *The Encyclopedia of the Dead*, history is the sum of human destinies, the totality of ephemeral happenings. That is why it records every action, every thought, every creative breath, every spot height in the survey, every shovelful of mud, every motion that cleared a brick from the ruins.

The post my father held after the war in the Land Office, which measured and registered the cadastre again from scratch, as happens after great historic upheavals, is accorded the detailed treatment it demands: quality of terrain, title deeds, new names for former German villages and new names for freshly colonized settlements. Nothing, as I say, is missing: the clay caking the rubber boots bought from a drunken soldier; a bad case of diarrhea caused by stuffed cabbage that had spoiled, at a bistro in Indjija; an affair with a Bosnian woman, a waitress, in Sombor; a bicycle accident near Čantavir and the bruised elbow that came of it; a night ride in a cattle car on the Senta–Subotica line; the purchase of a plump goose to take home for a New Year's celebration; a spree with some Russian engineers in Banovići; a molar pulled, outdoors, near a well sweep; a rally at which he got soaked to the bone; the death of Steva Bogdanov, surveyor, who stepped on a tripwire mine at the edge of some woods and with whom he had played billiards the previous day; the return of Aleksić, the stunt pilot, to the sky above Kalemegdan; serious alcohol poisoning in the village of Mrakodol; a ride in a crowded truck over the muddy road between Zrenjanin and Elemir; a dispute with a new boss, a man named Šuput, somewhere around Jaša Tomić; the purchase of a ton of Banovići coal after queuing from four in the morning at the Danube railway station, in –15°, the purchase

47

of a marble-top table at the flea market; a breakfast of 'American' cheese and powdered milk in the 'Bosnia' workers' canteen; his father's illness and death; the visit to the cemetery on the next Day of the Dead; a bitter quarrel with one Petar Janković and one Sava Dragović, who advocated the Stalinist line; their arguments and his counterarguments (which ended with my father's muffled 'F—— Stalin!').

Thus, the *Encyclopedia* immerses us in the atmosphere of the times, in its political realities.

The fear in which my father lived and the silence I myself remember – a heavy, oppressive silence – are construed by the book as infectious: one day he learned that that same Petar Janković, a colleague and distant relative, was reporting to the State Security Building every morning at six for a talk (as a result of having been denounced by the aforementioned Dragović), and would arrive at the office late, his face black and swollen from blows and lack of sleep; and on it went, every morning at sunrise for six months or so, until Petar recalled the names of some other people who shared his delusions about the Russians and listened to Radio Moscow.

Passing over the side streams – quarrels, reconciliations, spa visits (a whole family chronicle in miniature) – passing over the things that my father would bring home and that the *Encyclopedia* itemises with homely solicitude, I will mention only an Orion radio set, the *Collected Works* of Maxim Gorky, an oleander in an enormous wooden box, and a barrel for pickling cabbage, as I find them more important than the other trivia catalogued in the book, down to the lined fabric I bought for him with my first wages and the bottle of Martell cognac he drained in the course of a single evening.

But *The Encyclopedia of the Dead* is concerned with more than material goods: it is not a double-entry ledger or a catalogue, nor is it a list of names like the Book of Kings or Genesis, though it is that as well; it deals with spiritual matters, people's views of the world, of God, their doubts about the existence of the hereafter, their moral standards. Yet what is most amazing is its unique fusion of external and internal: it lays great stress on concrete facts, then creates a logical bond between the facts and man, or what we call man's soul. And whereas the compilers make no comment on certain objective particulars – the conversion of tile stoves to electricity (1969), the appearance of a bald spot on my father's head or his abrupt slide into gluttony, the refreshing elderberry drink he made from a recipe in *Politika* – they do interpret his sudden passion for stamp collecting in old age as compensation for his prolonged immobility. They have no doubt that peering at stamps through a magnifying glass represents, in part, the repressed fantasies so often lurking in staid, stable people with little proclivity for travel and adventure – the same frustrated petit-bourgeois romanticism that determined Father's attitude toward the sea. (He replaced journeys and distant horizons with more convenient, imaginary wanderings, using his first grandson's interest in the butterfly world of stamps as a pretext to keep from looking silly in other people's eyes and in his own.)

This, as you can see, is an area of the spiritual landscape quite near to the river's mouth, where friends' and relatives' funerals follow so closely on one another that every man – even one less inclined than my father to silent meditation – turns philosopher, insofar as philosophy is the contemplation of the meaning of human existence.

Dissatisfied with his life, rankled by the melancholy of old age that nothing can assuage, neither devoted children nor affectionate grandchildren nor the relative calm of everyday life, he started grumbling and getting drunk more often. When he drank, he burst into fits of anger quite unexpected in so mild a man with such a gentle smile. He would curse

God, heaven, earth, the Russians, the Americans, the Germans, the government, and all those responsible for granting him such a miserable pension after he had slaved a lifetime, but most of all he cursed television, which filled his dreary evenings by bringing into his house – with an impudence verging on rudeness – the grand illusion of life.

The next day, himself again and mutely contrite, he would feed the goldfinch on the balcony, talk to it, whistle to it, lifting the cage high above his head as if brandishing a lantern in the murk of human tribulations. Or, taking off his pajamas at last, he would dress with a groan, put on his hat, and walk to Takovska Street, to the main post office, and buy stamps. Then, in the afternoon, sipping coffee while perched on the edge of an armchair, his grandson at his side, he would arrange the stamps in albums with the help of delicate tweezers.

Occasionally, in moments of despair, he regretted his past life, wailing as old people do: how God never granted him a proper schooling, how he would go to his grave ignorant, never tasting the finer things in life, never seeing the seas and cities of the world, never knowing the things that rich and educated people know.

And his journey to Trieste ended as ingloriously as his trip to Rovinj.

It was, in his sixty-sixth year, his first border crossing, and it, too, took a good deal of pushing and pulling. Nor were his arguments any easier to counter: an intelligent person did not go to a country whose language he did not know; he had no intention of making a fortune on the black market; he had no craving for macaroni or Chianti and would much prefer an everyday Mostar *žilavka* or a Prokuplje white, at home.

Nevertheless we persuaded him to apply for a passport.

He came back ill-humored, ill-tempered, crushed: he had had a falling out with Mother (the shoes she had bought him leaked and pinched), and the police had searched them and ransacked their luggage on the return trip to Belgrade.

Need I mention that the visit to Trieste – the downpour, with Father under the awning of the Hotel Adriatico without an umbrella, lost, like a bedraggled old dog, while Mother rummaged through shoes by the Ponte Rosso – receives in the *Encyclopedia* the coverage an episode of the sort deserves? His only consolation during the whole wretched excursion came from buying some flower seeds outside a shop there. (Fortunately, the packets had pictures of the flowers on them and clearly marked prices, so he did not need to haggle with the saleswoman.) By then D.M. had become quite 'involved in cultivating decorative flowers,' as the *Encyclopedia* puts it. (It continues with an inventory of the flowers in pots and window boxes on the front and rear balconies.)

He had simultaneously begun to fill his time by painting floral patterns all over the house, a kind of floral contagion. This sudden explosion of artistic talent came as a surprise. Dissatisfied – as he was dissatisfied with everything – with the way a retired officer, an amateur housepainter, had whitewashed the bathroom (singing 'The Partisans' March' all day long to pace his brushstrokes) leaving behind large, unevenly covered portions, my father rolled up his sleeves and set doggedly to work. Having failed to remove the dark spots on the wall, he decided to camouflage them with oil paint, following the outlines of the moisture stains. And thus the first flower – a gigantic bellflower or a lily, heaven only knows what it was – came into being.

We all praised him. The neighbors dropped in to view his handiwork. Even his favorite grandson expressed sincere admiration. That was how it all started. Next came the bathroom window, which he covered with tiny cornflower-blue posies, but he left them slanted and unfinished, so that the design, painted directly on the glass, gave the illusion of a windblown curtain.

From then on, he painted all day, unflaggingly, a cigarette dangling from his lips. (And in the silence we could hear the wheezing of his lungs, like bellows.) He painted flowers that bore little resemblance to real flowers, painted them all over old scratched trunks, china lampshades, cognac bottles, plain glass vases, Nescafé jars, and wooden cigar boxes. On the aquamarine background of a large soda-water siphon he painted the names of Belgrade cafés in the lettering he had once used for islands on maps: The Brioni, The Gulf of Kotor, The Seagull, The Sailor, The Daybreak, Café Serbia, The Vidin Gate, The Istanbul Gate, The Skadarlija, The Three Hats, The Two Deer, Under the Linden, Three Bunches of Grapes, The Šumatovac, The Seven Days, The March on the Drina, The Kalemegdan, The Kolarac, The Homeland, The Plowman, The Obrenovac, The Oplenac, The Town of Dušan, The River's Mouth, The Smederevo, The Hunter's Horn, The Question Mark, The Last Chance.

The curious fact that he died on his first grandson's twelfth birthday did not escape the compilers' attention. Nor did they fail to note his resistance to our naming his last grandson after him. We thought that we were indulging his vanity and that he would take it as a sign of special attention and favor, but all he did was grumble and I could see in his eyes a glimmer of the terror that would flash behind his glasses a year later when the certainty of the end suddenly dawned on him. The succession of the quick and the dead, the universal myth of the chain of generations, the vain solace man invents to make the thought of dying more acceptable – in that instant my father experienced them all as an insult; it was as though by the magical act of bestowing his name upon a newborn child, no matter how much his flesh and blood, we were 'pushing him into the grave.' I did not yet know that he had discovered a suspicious growth in the area of his groin and believed, or perhaps even knew for sure, that, like a tuber, a strange, poisonous plant was sprouting in his intestines.

One of the last chapters of the *Encyclopedia* details the funeral ceremony: the name of the priest who administered the last rites, a description of the wreaths, a list of the people who accompanied him from the chapel, the number of candles lit for his soul, the text of the obituary in *Politika*.

The oration delivered over the bier by Nikola Bešević, a Land Office colleague of many years' standing ('Comrade Djuro served his fatherland with equal honor before the war, during the occupation, and after the war in the period of the revitalization and reconstruction of our ravaged and sorely afflicted country'), is given in full, because, despite certain exaggerations and platitudes, despite lapses in rhetoric, Bešević's oration over the body of his dead comrade and fellow countryman clearly exemplified something of the message and principles represented by the great *Encyclopedia of the Dead* ('His memory shall live forever and ever. Praise and glory be unto him!').

Well, that is more or less the end, where my notes stop. I shall not cite the sorry inventory of items he left behind: shirts, passport, documents, eyeglasses (the light of day glistening painfully in empty lenses just removed from their case) – in other words, the items passed on to my mother, at the hospital, the day after his death. It is all painstakingly set down in the *Encyclopedia*; not a single handkerchief is missing, not the Morava cigarettes or the issue of *Ilustrovana Politika* with a crossword puzzle partly completed in his hand.

Then come the names of the doctors, nurses, and visitors, the day and hour of the operation (when Dr Petrović cut him open and sewed him shut, realizing it was useless to operate: the sarcoma had spread to the vital organs). I haven't the strength to describe the look he gave me as he said goodbye on the hospital stairs a day or two before the operation; it contained an entire lifetime and all the terror that comes of knowing death. *Everything a living man can know of death.*

So, frozen through and in tears, I managed in those few hours to look through all the pages in his entry. I had no idea of time. Had I spent an hour in the icy library, or was day breaking outside? As I say, I lost all track of time and place. I hastened to put down as much information as possible; I wanted some evidence, for my hours of despair, that my father's life had not been in vain, that there were still people on earth who record and accord value to every life, every affliction, every human existence. (Meager consolation, but consolation nonetheless.)

Suddenly, somewhere in the final pages devoted to him, I noticed a flower, an unusual flower, that I first took for a vignette or the schematic drawing of a plant preserved in the world of the dead as an example of extinct flora. The caption, however, indicated that it was the *basic* floral pattern in my father's drawings. My hands trembling, I began to copy it. More than anything it resembled a gigantic peeled and cloven orange, crisscrossed with fine red lines like capillaries. For a moment I was disappointed. I was familiar with all the drawings my father had done at leisure on walls, boards, bottles and boxes, and none was anything like this one. Yes, I said to myself, even *they* can make a mistake. And then, after copying the gigantic peeled orange into my notebook, I read the final paragraph and let out a scream. I awoke drenched in sweat. I immediately wrote down all of the dream I remembered. And this is what remains of it. . .

Do you know what was in the last paragraph? That D.M. took up painting at the time the first symptoms of cancer appeared. And that therefore his obsession with floral patterns coincided with the progress of the disease.

When I showed the drawing to Dr Petrović, he confirmed, with some surprise, that it looked exactly like the sarcoma in my father's intestine. And that the *efflorescence* had doubtless gone on for years.

The Legend of the Sleepers

They stayed in their cave three hundred years, increased by nine.

KORAN, XVIII:25

1

They lay on their backs on rough, damp haircloth that was somewhat mildewed from the humidity and had worn through in places from their movements, their twitching, their bones wherever their bodies were in contact with the camel hair – at the back of the head, at shoulder blades and elbows, near a protruding pelvis, beneath heels and calves rigid as distaffs.

They lay on their backs, with their hands crossed in prayer like corpses, on damp and rotting haircloth that had worn thin beneath their bodies from the rare unconscious twitching of weary sleepers, sleepers weary of life and movement but sleepers nonetheless; for their limbs did move, though imperceptibly to the human eye, and the haircloth beneath them had worn thin in places where it had been pressed against the rock of the cave by the weight of their sleep and their stonelike bodies, where it had been exposed to the stirring of human clay, the chafing of bones on the dank haircloth, and the haircloth rubbing on the diamantine rock of the cave.

They lay on their backs in the tranquil repose of great sleepers, but the movements of their limbs in the darkness of time wore thin the wet haircloth beneath them, gnawing at the fibers of the camel hair, which were abraded imperceptibly, as when water, coupled with time, begins to bore into the hard heart of stone.

They lay on their backs in a dark cave on Mount Celius, with their hands crossed in prayer like corpses, all three of them, Dionysius and his friend Malchus and, a short distance away, John, the saintly shepherd, and his dog, Qitmir.

Beneath their eyelids burdened by sleep, their eyelids anointed with the balsam and hemlock of sleep, the greenish crescents of their dead eyes did not show through, for the darkness was too profound, the dank darkness of time, the murk of the cave of eternity.

From the walls and vaults of the cave, eternal water dripped drop by drop and flowed in a barely audible murmur through the veins of the rocks like the blood in the veins of the sleepers, and from time to time a drop fell on their torpid bodies, on their stone-like faces, and ran down the wrinkles in their foreheads into the shell of an ear, lingered in the curved wrinkles of an eyelid, trickled across a greenish eyeball like an icy tear, or halted on the lashes of a petrified eye. Yet they did not awaken.

Deaf, their ears plugged by the lead of sleep and the pitch of darkness, they lay motionless, staring into the darkness of their beings, the darkness of time and eternity, which had turned their sleeping hearts to stone, which had halted their breath and the movement of their lungs, which had frozen the murmur of blood in their veins.

The only thing that grew – nourished by the moisture of the cave and the immobility of the bodies, stimulated by the ashes of oblivion and the frenzy of dreams – was the hair on their heads and the stubble on their faces, the fuzz on their bodies and the fuzz under their arms; the only thing that grew in their sleep – invisibly, as water builds and destroys invisibly – were their nails, crackling.

2

The youngest, Dionysius, who had a rose at his heart and who lay between his friend Malchus and John the shepherd, was the first to wake, suddenly, as if touched by the wind of time and memory. The first thing he heard was the dripping of water from the vaults of the cave; the first thing he felt was a thorn in his heart. Immersed in silence, his consciousness, a weary sleeper's consciousness steeped in the dank darkness of the cave, was unable to collect itself at once, for his body was torpid from long repose and his soul was clouded by dreams.

In his soul he calls out the name of the Lord his God, calls out the sweet name of his Prisca, and remembers everything that happened, recalled it with the horror of a man dying and the joy of a man in love. For what happened to his soul and his body – he no longer knows when – seemed once more like a dream; perhaps it was no more than a dream now, a nightmare of life and a nightmare of death, a nightmare of unrequited love, a nightmare of time and eternity.

To the left and right he felt the bodies of his friend Malchus and John the shepherd smitten with a dead sleep; he felt them even though they slept without breath or movement, as mute as mummies, lacking even the odor of human bodies, the smell of human decay; he felt the presence of their disembodied essence, sensed, somewhere to the right, near John's legs, the disembodied, mummified body of the shepherd's dog, its front paws extended, lying at its master's side and keeping a life-and-death watch over his dead sleep.

3

His stone-like body, his torpid limbs still stretched out on the frayed haircloth whose moisture he did not feel, Dionysius painfully separates the fingers of his crossed hands, fingers so stiff from sleep and immobility that they seemed to have grown together, and he remembers his body and his bodily existence, remembers his heart, which – lo! – has come alive in him, as had his innards and his lungs and his eyes sealed by the lead of sleep and his member, cold and sleeping, as distant as sin was distant from him.

And he returns his consciousness to the heart of the cave, to its clotted pitch-black darkness, and listens for the eternal clepsydra of time, for he wished his bodiless being to inhabit time, his consciousness and his body to inhabit the heart of time once again, and return to the time before this dream and this cave. And first he remembers Prisca's sweet name, for she had been in his dreams and his reality, in his own heart and the heart of time, in the heart of sleep and the heart of waking.

At first he did not know what to do, as he did not wish to awaken his weary, somnolent companions, his accomplices in dreams, and he plunged with his own consciousness into the river of time to separate dream from reality, to grasp – with the aid of his consciousness and his memories, with the aid of his Lord God to whom he prayed – what had happened.

Yet there was nothing in him but memories of his own dream and his awakening, what had been and what was now; there was still nothing in him but the indissoluble darkness prevailing before the Creation, before Genesis, when the Lord had not yet divided light from darkness and day from night, when the Lord had not yet distinguished dream from reality and reality from dream.

And had it not been for the rose at his heart, the sweet name of Prisca, her memory etched in his body, her presence in his heart, his skin, his consciousness, his empty innards, he would not have awoken at all.

4

For she was no longer the Prisca of old, the Prisca of his bygone dreams, the Prisca he had found at the gates of his recent sleep, in the heart of his recent awakening. Alas, she was no longer the Prisca unto whom he had made eternal vows, no longer his Prisca of earlier dreams and an earlier reality; she was not – God forgive him – the same woman, the daughter of Emperor Decius, enemy of Christianity, or the same dream of the same woman; she was not his Prisca, who had pledged herself to him for all eternity; she was another woman with Prisca's name and very like her yet not the same Prisca, similar to her in shape, but no, not she.

And he conjured up the living, all too painfully living memory of her image, the image of his Prisca, but now it was the image of two women merged by time and memory into one, without limits or bounds, for they were made of the dust and ashes of two memories, the clay of two successive creations into which sleep had breathed a soul, his soul.

And the two images solidified in his consciousness, his memory, and he kneaded the clay of which they were made, and in the end he could no longer distinguish two women, two dreams, but only one, Prisca of the almond eyes, his Prisca, present and past, and the memory fills him with joy and strength, enough to wrest him from sleep yet not enough to move his torpid limbs, for he is overcome with fear of his own thoughts at the very moment that he winds up the thread of remembrance and remembers everything that happened before this sleep.

5

And he sees the light of the torches, which shine down like stars from the vault of the cave above their heads, and he remembers and hears the murmur of the throng that gathered around them and then the silence that reigned for a moment and the shout and flight of the crowd when John, the saintly shepherd, raises his arms to heaven and calls out the name of the Lord.

Was it a dream? Was it the dream of a sleepwalker, a dream within a dream, and hence more real than a real dream, since it cannot be measured against waking, since it cannot be measured by consciousness, because it is a dream from which one awakens into another dream? Or was it a god-like dream, a dream of time and eternity? A dream without illusions and doubts, a dream with its own language and senses, a dream of both soul and body, a dream of consciousness and corporality both, a dream with clear-cut boundaries, with its own language and sound, a dream that is palpable, that can be explored with taste, smell, and hearing, a dream stronger than waking, a dream such as only the dead perhaps can dream, a dream that cannot be denied by a razor nicking your chin, for blood flows at once, and everything you do is further proof of reality and waking; skin and heart bleed alike in the dream, the body rejoices in the dream as does the soul, the only miracle in this dream is life itself; awakening from this dream means awakening into death.

They had no time even for leave-taking, for each of them was absorbed in his soul and his forgiveness, and each to himself and then all in unison they began whispering prayers with their dry lips, for they knew the throng would return and had left only to summon Decius's legionaries or prepare the cages of wild animals, putting guards at the entrance of the cave until all is ready for their slaughter, which the populace, the godless multitude, will relish.

6

And they came again bearing torches and lanterns that illumined the cave with a new and powerful light, came chanting songs and psalms, and with children bearing candles and icons, and the cave was illumined with their pious song and prayers, the voices of the priests resounding among the rocks, the voices of the children, all boys in white, like a choir of heavenly hosts.

Before long, the cave fills with the smoke of torches and the fragrance of incense, and everyone sang the glory of the Lord in a loud voice; the priests and the children and the three of them, Dionysius, Malchus, and John, the saintly shepherd, they all sang psalms to the glory of Jesus the Nazarene, the miracle worker and redeemer.

Was that, too, a dream? Was it a vision, or were they at the heavenly gates? Was it the end of a nightmare and dream, or was it their ascension to heaven?

He gazed on them with a troubled soul, as those in the gallery gazed upon the three men. And in the light of the torches he sees their faces and their raiment, and he was greatly surprised to find that they were scarlet and crimson, made of sheepskin dyed red, trimmed in gold and silver and bronze. And before them they held icons gleaming with gold and silver and precious stones.

7

Then several muscular young men stand forward from the crowd, bow before them, and, after making the sign of the cross and kissing their hands and feet, lift them one by one, as effortlessly as if they were children, and carry them across the cave's rocky floor, holding them carefully, like icons, barely touching them with their powerful hands, while the crowd lit their steps and their way, still singing to the glory of the Lord.

At the head of the procession they carried John, the saintly shepherd, his hands clasped in prayer, whispering his simple prayer, which God prefers to all others; next they carried Malchus, who had a long, white beard and was arrayed, like John, in bright robes embroidered with gold; and last, rocking slightly in the powerful arms of his bearers as in a boat, came Dionysius.

Was that, too, a dream?

And he sees the shaved heads of the young men on whose shoulders the litter conveying his body rested, a body he too felt was as light as that of a child or a feeble old man. This ascension – was it, too, a dream? And this singing and the eyes of the young men carrying him, who dared not gaze up at him, so that all he saw were thick eyebrows beneath low foreheads and lashes below half-shut lids; the bare, powerful necks and, lit by a ray of light, the crowns of the heads of those carrying Malchus before him as they mounted a slope, moving closer to the sky and the heavenly paradise, while the crowd standing on either side of them lifted torches and lanterns high above their heads, and he, not daring to look them in the eye, not even for an instant, lest he find beneath the half-shut lids the vacant, greenish eyeballs of insensible sleepwalkers who wander in their sleep and chant psalms and prayers, who in their deep slumber, their wandering slumber, carry the three of them past the cave's stone whirlpools, down deep gorges and up slippery cliffs, across vast, capacious halls and temples of crystal foam, through narrow passageways beneath low vaults.

And whence their sure step, the sublime composure with which they skirt all dangers, carrying their load with skill and grace, barely touching it with their powerful hands?

In vain did he try to dispel his doubts, to find a gaze, a human eye in which to glimpse his face, in which to discover his image, proof that he was awake. If only he can catch the eye of a child, one of the angels in white robes standing above him on either side of the path, to both left and right, in the crystal gallery, as in a temple – but in vain. No sooner does he think one of the children was glancing at him with its angelic, human eyes, no sooner does he think one of them sought his glance, no sooner does he turn his eyes in its direction than it turns its gaze away, lowering the curtain of its leaden lids and opaque lashes while continuing to sing its song and, eyes now tightly shut, to open its round mouth like a fish, and he, Dionysius, feels a certain hypocrisy in that hidden glance, that fish-like mouth, a deliberate withholding, a fear or respect, or the torpor of a sleepwalker.

For only sleepwalkers can move as they moved, sleepwalkers led over the abyss by a sovereign hand, by the daring of people who do not see the deep chasm beneath their feet and the madness of people sustained by the power of their ancient divinity, the pagan power of bodies that still recall the faith of ancestors who bowed down to the moon, their procession and their outstretched arms a tribute to Luna, pagan goddess of the moon, whence the souls of their departed call down to them, for that procession is merely the call of blood and the call of time. And he dared not utter a word, lest he should awaken the slumbering pagans, the sleepwalkers, who had gathered in the cave to celebrate their festival, to honor their pagan goddess – for surely a full moon is shining outside.

8

And he dared not utter a word save the prayer he whispered to himself, scarcely moving his lips, for he feared he would awaken from his sleepwalking enchantment and send them all toppling into the murky depths over which they now bore him, treading barefoot and all but soundlessly through the dank cave, which sparkled with glistening drops; his voice and his awakening would have drawn them all back into the murky chasm out of which the sleepwalkers are now carrying them, up the slope, higher and higher, and in their fear of awakening they would all have toppled into the abyss yawning below them, deep into the dark bowels of the cave, which not even the light of the torches can reach but whose depths and precipices are present in his waking, sleepwalking consciousness. And he hears a stone fall beneath the bare feet of those carrying him, hears it tumbling down, skipping from rock to rock, fleet and resonant, then more hesitant and hushed, retreating like an echo, but the sound never ceased, it merely faded, for it did not touch bottom any more than did his half-wakeful, half-dormant consciousness.

Is it a dream or a sleepwalking illusion of his half-dormant consciousness, a dream of his pagan body, descending as it did from pagan ancestors, worshippers of the moon goddess, the full-moon goddess, ancestors who are calling to him now. Surely there is a full moon outside or a new moon at least, and the souls of his ancestors are awakening, the souls of his ancient forebears, calling to his pagan body, tempting his pagan blood.

Or is it the ascension of his soul to heaven, the moment when soul shears away from body, Christian soul from pagan body, sinful body from sinful soul, to which mercy is granted, whose sins are forgiven?

Are they a dream, the dog carried next to John, cradled like the Lamb of God, and the boy pressing the dog Qitmir to his bosom like a sacrificial lamb or pagan idol and carrying it over gorges and ravines, clasping it to his heart like the Good Shepherd, his eyes pinned to the ground, venturing not so much as a glance into Qitmir's cloudy green-blue eyes veiled by the cataracts of sleep, eyes green and blue like plums, eyes half open, all but extinguished and blind. Nor does he, Dionysius, dare catch Qitmir's eye now that the boy with the dog has paused at his side to let the litter bearers, hugging the ground and virtually on all fours, through the narrow passage; and he, Dionysius, feels as though he were hovering above the rocks, always in the same position, half reclining, his head slightly raised and resting on the chest of one of his bearers; and he hears only the bearers' quiet, restrained breathing. The boy and the dog have disappeared, for the boy paused before the narrow neck of the cave to let through the men who are carrying the three of them, that is, John, Malchus, and himself, Dionysius; the boy, his eyes pinned to the ground, remained behind at the entrance to the narrow cleft in the cave to wait his turn, still clutching the blue-eyed Qitmir in his arms.

9

Light flickered in from both ends of the narrow passageway, behind him barely visible, ahead of him, at the end of the tunnel, brighter and brighter, filtering through the sharp teeth of Polyphemus' massive, gaping jaws, for such it clearly was: the entry to the cave of long ago, and he remembers it now as he remembers the story John the saintly shepherd told him then, in that first dream or first reality. The passageway has been widened, or so it seems to him, and he could see from the shoulders of his bearers that the wall of the cave had been smoothed over at this point, he could see the gaping jaw and its broken eyeteeth, shiny, even, white and crystalline at the tip, with fresh diagonal notches, absolutely white and as dazzling as salt, on short rust-colored stumps.

Was that, too, a dream?

And the cripples who started swarming about their feet, wriggling like worms, kissing their hands and feet even before their strong bearers managed to carry them out of the cave. And the entrance to the cave, which he remembered well for its desecrated vaults and the drawings that shepherds had scratched into the hard stone with rocks or knives – for there had once been false idols and asses' heads drawn on the walls by the sinful hands of shepherds, and, as high as the human hand could reach, lewd figures, and there had been the stench of human excrement.

And now – lo! – the lewd figures and asses' heads have been erased, though fresh traces of scraping and filing are still visible on the rock, and the smell of human excrement has evaporated, they must have cleaned it up; there are now lanterns and fragrant torches hanging from chinks in the walls of the cave, the vault is covered with flowers and laurel wreaths and icons inlaid with gold, and the floor is spread with a carpet of flowers, now trampled by the bare feet of the litter bearers while the people sing psalms and whisper prayers.

The blind and the crippled, wriggling like worms, swarm about his feet, kissing his body and begging in words muffled and horrible, begging him in the name of love and faith, the sun and the moon, life and death, heaven and hell, begging and imploring him to restore their sight, heal their wounds and deadened limbs, restore the light of day and the light of faith.

Are they a dream or a nightmare, the cripples begging for alms, the poor wretches who beat one another with their crutches and scratch one another's eyes out for the mercy of his body, for the mercy of being healed – is this a dream? His impotence to utter a word to them, to do a thing for them, these poor wretches, these cripples whom the muscular young men remove from the path of the procession, pushing them aside, blind and frail, lame and paralyzed – is this a dream? His impotence to grasp it all, the miracle, the suffering, his own impotence, his helplessness to do anything for the wretches who beg and plead with him, to tell them of his helplessness, to ask for *their* mercy, for a human word, to implore them to believe him, believe in his impotence, to win them over with curses and entreaties so that they can tell him what is happening to him, whether it is all a dream, those dead, blind eyes turning to him, vacant and gruesome, rolling, bloody and gruesome, those blind eyes seeking him out and finding him, for they are the only eyes he saw, the only eyes that turned to him, that took pity and turned to him, for not even the cripples who drag themselves up to him on their stumps to kiss his feet with their icy lips, not even they granted him a glance, they too embrace him and plead with him without looking at him, raising only their mutilated arms in a half embrace and clasping their stumps in a gruesome half prayer that ends at the elbows – in the misshapen wrinkles and seams of mutilated half limbs.

Is it a nightmare, is it his ascension to heaven? Is it a nightmare of the purgatory through which his body must pass, is it the final punishment, the final admonition to a sinful body, that spectacle of human horror which serves the soul, before its ascension, by reminding it of hell?

Is it a nightmare or perhaps only the Calvary of his body and soul, hell itself where they are taking his body to be roasted and quartered, and the prayers, the heavenly singing, the light and the procession by shoulder, on the wings of angels, were these nothing but the last temptation of a sinful soul so the soul will recall paradise lost, the gardens of paradise and delights of paradise of which it is not worthy, the Lord bearing him past these gardens on the wings of fallen angels that his soul might experience rapture and bliss, experience the fragrance of incense and myrrh, the balm of prayer, in order to suffer the torments of hell more acutely, for prayers and hymns will ring in the soul's memory, the fragrances of fragrant torches and incense will live in the soul's memory, the light will live on in remembrance, a glimmer of heavenly light?

10

Is it a dream? Is the daylight a dream, the daylight that floods him when the people move away from the entrance to the cave, when a door opened in the wall of the crowd standing around and a new light appeared, without doubt divine, a forgotten light, at once remote and close, the light of a sunlit day, the light of life and clear sight?

At first there was nothing but the blue vault of the sky, far off, luminous in its own glow, sky-blue, far above his head, a sky-blue sea, calm and serene, swelled by high tide; then in the mild blue of the sky he thinks he can see a few white clouds, not heavenly sheep, not a flock, a white, heavenly flock out to graze, but wisps of white wool floating with the tide of the blue vault, just enough to keep the human eye, his eye, from doubting the blue of the sky, just enough to keep his soul from wandering.

For this was without doubt the light of God's day and it was without doubt the blue light of the sky or the light of his ascension to heaven. Or was this too a dream, the flash that shut his eyes before he was quite out of the cave, rocking on the carriers' powerful shoulders as in a boat, the light spattering him like water, his soul sinking into the glittering blue wave as into holy water, neck deep, the light engulfing him in a warm bliss that emanated from a distant memory of his soul, a distant vision, the light lashing at his eyes like an illumination and like the flame of angels' wings, while he presses his eyes shut, presses until they ache, not from the darkness now or the visions but from the light? And he feels the difference, feels it behind his tightly shut eyes, for in his consciousness, somewhere in the middle of his forehead, somewhere behind the frontal bone, in the center, there between his eyes, at the base of the optic nerve and at the heart of vision itself, purple disks began to quiver, purple and crimson, and blue and yellow and green, then red again, and it was without doubt light and not an illusion, or perhaps only an optical illusion, but it was light!

11

Unless that too, alas, was a dream, a bodily illusion, an optical illusion, the illusion of a sleepwalker who has overstepped the bounds and borders of night and moon, of daybreak and moonlight, and stepped into day and the light of the rising sun, the eternal divinity in eternal conflict with the goddess Luna, and now – lo! – coming to disperse the illusory, the specious light of the deposed goddess, its much hated foe; but it was light! Not the flickering, feeble light that gnaws and chafes itself, ignites and snuffs itself, pursues and smothers itself, consuming itself in its own flame and smoke, its own quiver and flight, its own coals and embers; yes, truly it was light!

Not cold moonlight but broad daylight, the light of the sun piercing his tightly shut lids, a crimson flame infiltrating the thick mat of his lashes, the pores of his skin, the light of day felt on each part of the body that emerged from the cold darkness of the cave, a warm light and salutary, the life-giving light of God's day!

Unless that too, alas, was a dream?

The crimson rushing into his blood, his heart pounding, and the blood coursing through his body, warm and jubilant, blood suddenly crimson and vigorous; the warm mantle of sun he wrapped around himself as if it were his own warm skin, a light gold mantle of sun covering his body, his icy wet hairshirt overlain with sumptuous silk.

Or was this, too, a dream, the new earthly scent penetrating his nostrils long dulled by sleep and repose, the warm scent of the earth, the scent of grass, of vegetation, the blessed breath of light and life which after the musty air of the cave was as sweet as an apple?

Could that too have been a dream? The blessed libation of his spirit and his body, the blaze that kept him from opening his eyes, for it smote him on the forehead with such force that the light turned to darkness, red and yellow, blue and crimson and green darkness, and he had to keep his eyes tight shut, for the warm red darkness behind his eyelids made him feel as if he had plunged his head into boiling sacrificial blood.

12

Like a child in its cradle or on its mother's back, he rocked on the shoulders of his carriers – a child asleep on its mother's back, in a field, the sun beating down, eyes closed in blissful languor, feeling only the warmth of the sunlight on its skin, on its heavy limbs, through its tightly shut lids.

Stunned by the great light and the smells, on the border between consciousness and unconsciousness, he listened to the prayers and chants of the pilgrims, the angelic chorus of children's voices, and the squeal of instruments, the whine of the citharas, the pipes' lament, and let the resounding anthems and angels' trumpet blasts flow over him.

Washed with ever-multiplying voices, voices of the crowd, lamentations and sobs, curses and entreaties, borne on the wings of ever-multiplying smells, smells of the crowd and of sweat penetrating his nostrils at the moment when warm red blood of the sun starts streaming through the iceberg of his body embalmed by clammy darkness, he suddenly catches the odor of his carriers, the odor of their shaven heads and pungent armpits, and then the forgotten odor of cattle as they were lifted, all three of them, onto an ox-drawn cart spread with a soft sheepskin.

His head propped on soft pillows, he lay in the cart as in a boat and listened to the creak of the wheels, slow and lazy, mingled with chanting and wailing. Once, half opening his tightly shut lids, letting in the daylight, which made a painful incision in the eyeball, like a steel blade, he looked about him, to left and right, and saw the faces of his friend Malchus and of John, mute, expressionless faces, like his own face undoubtedly, saw them staring, like him, with half-open eyes at the blue of the firmament, the wonder of creation.

Was that, too, a dream? The warm motionlessness and sudden calm, the child-like, animal-like submission to sun and daylight, and the eyes turned toward the vault of heaven, heaven's blue vault, now cloudless, the oblivion-blue, regeneration-blue, miracle-blue vault of heaven. Was that, too, a dream?

And he felt the joy of his body after the dank, slimy, viscid shell of darkness has fallen away, the childlike joy of the flesh, of entrails and bones, a joy of bone marrow and brain marrow, a bestial amphibian joy, a reptilian joy, when the body in labour delivers itself from the slough of darkness, the shell of dankness and moisture, the brittle skin of damp and timeless blackness that seeps through pores, damp and timeless, to the sensitive, bloody layer beneath the skin and, like a serpent's venom, permeates the body, its flesh and bones and bone marrow, following the same paths as the cart and the warm light of the sun.

Was this too a dream? The sunbath wringing darkness from the marrow of his bones, the fumes rising from his body as it oozed the serpent's green venom through its pores, making room for the light of life, the life-giving sap that would make his blood red again.

Was that, too, a dream, the moment when the heavy rocks of his cave-tomb opened before him and he was dazzled by heavenly light?

13

Back in the darkness of the cave, he could recollect it all with painful clarity, for his icy body remembered the warmth, his blood remembered the light, his eye remembered the blue of the heavens, his ear recalled the singing and the pipes.

And now, behold! All was silence again, all was eclipse again, all was torpor and numbness, absence of movement and absence of light, yet he remembers *the light*, remembers it with a shudder of carnal yearning, the very memory of it makes him quiver, as when the sun light touched him in that dream or that reality, the sun perched on his shoulders, embraced his loins, when in that dream or that reality the sun sowed its seed in his viscera, rippled through his blood, warmed his bones.

And now – behold! – all is once again nothing but a tomb of the body and a dungeon of the soul, a realm of darkness, a palace of mold, green mold, infusing his heart and skin, bone marrow and brain marrow, and in vain he reaches out to touch the moist and icy stone of the cave with his dry, swollen fingers, in vain does he lift his eyelids, in vain touch them with his fingers to test whether it was not all a dream, an illusion, the silence dotted with the dripping of invisible drops from the invisible vaults of the cave, the darkness riddled by a muted murmur, in vain does he strain to hear the singing and the whine of the pipes, the singing that he remembered so vividly, that his body remembers.

Nothing. Nothing but the empty echo of memory and the resonant silence of the cave; the sound of silence, the stillness of time. The light of darkness. The water of dream. Water.

14

Jolting along, the cart entered the town, and high above his head rose the vaults of the town gates, cleaving the blue of the heavens with their white stone arches, bridges spanning invisible banks, stone arches within reach of the hands lying motionless at the sides of his numb, all but lifeless body.

Here and there, where the stone had cracked, a blade of grass sprouted from the arches, two or three blades of green grass, or some roots, white and split down the middle, or the rust-colored frond of a wild fern emerging from the heart of the stone. No, it was no dream! The sun streaked with shadows beneath the arches of the town gates, the fern, the grass, the moss within each of his hands – no, surely it was not a dream.

For one can dream water, fire, and sky; one can dream man and woman, especially woman; one can dream dreams in reality and dreams in a dream; but surely this was not a dream, this white chiseled stone, these vaults, this fortress town.

15

Creaking and jolting, the ox-drawn cart took them under the arches of the town gates and through the shadows of the houses lining the streets, yet he barely saw the houses, for he stared straight up, his eyes glassy and motionless with wonder or sleep, merely sensing the stone presence of the stone houses, the lofty houses, on either side of him, left and right, whenever a shadow fell on his face and tired eyes, but he also sensed the stone presence of the tumbledown huts, which did not block the sun but were no less present, invisible but solid and real, more real than the sky above his head, more real than the creak of the yoke and the voices of the crowd still accompanying them, murmuring prayers and singing psalms.

16

'O thou who art blessed, thou shalt stand before the Emperor!' No, it was no dream. He could still recall the voice, perhaps not the face, but the voice bursting with exaltation, a voice cracking with fear or fervor. 'O thou who art blessed!'

And lying there motionless, in the cart, he saw the red beard and light blue eyes of a young man leaning over him, from behind, in such a way that his face, upside down, hovered directly above him and blocked the sun. 'O thou who art blessed!' Was the young man saying that to him, Dionysius, or were dream and reality still toying with his consciousness?

Staring into the young man's eyes, he noted with mistrust that they were observing and following his own, timidly and apprehensively perhaps, but with a certain youthful insolence.

And looking up at him mutely, Dionysius saw his thin lips and red beard begin to move, and he read the words from those lips before his ears brought them to his consciousness: 'O thou who art blessed!'

Was it not mockery and scorn? Was it not the voice of his dream, the voice of his illusions?

And Dionysius said, 'Who art thou?' – his voice emerging abruptly, scarcely audible. The insolence in those light blue eyes now seemed to have vanished, and the young man quickly turned away, his red-tipped eyelashes coming down over his eyes and his lips beginning to move again.

'O thou who art blessed! I am thy slave and the slave of thy master!'

Were they, too, a dream? Those stuttering lips, that quivering beard?

'Decius is not my master!' he uttered, expecting a lion's roar in return. But lo! just as he closed his eyes the better to hear the lion roar, the face of the young man with the red beard vanished, leaving only the vast heavens spread out above him.

17

All at once there was silence, broken only by the monotonous singing and keening of the people: the creak of the wheels jolting along the bumpy, winding road had ceased; the cart had come to a halt.

Was that, too, a dream? The calm suddenly descending upon his soul after a long muddle of voices and strange happenings – was that, too, a dream? The voices of the crowd had died down to nothing, and the creak of the cart had ceased, and the whine and scrape of the wheels. The sun's rays, which until then had fallen at an angle on his face, were gone, screened by an awning he could not see. His body rested on a soft sheepskin, and the odor of wool seeped into his nostrils, and the odor of cypress and the odor of the sun-drenched day and the warm, intoxicating odors of the sea.

Lulled until then, like an infant in its cradle, by the whine of the wheels and the sway of the cart, his numb body, his light bones, his empty innards, his quiet heart, his dry skin all surrendered to the serenity of easy breathing; he felt like a child who had just been awakened.

No, it was no dream – that serenity, that radiance!

18

Even before looking to left and right, even before wondering whether it was all a dream, even before apprehending the miraculous ascension of his body in this scented bath of a summer's day, he remembered sweet Prisca's name and at once his body was flooded with bliss and the air with the scent of roses.

Oh, joy!

And the mere recollection of his body and heart during that moment of serenity, that wave of exaltation, there, before the palace gate, when the voices of the crowd had died down and the creak of the cart had ceased, when Prisca's sweet name is engraved on his soul and exudes a rose-like aroma – now, once more, in the darkness of the cave, the tomb of eternity, it awakens in him a vague and distant elation, grazing him with its breath, and his body is flooded with light and heat from afar; but then all returns to anguish of the spirit and the darkness of time.

19

He lay in the darkness of the cave, vainly straining his eyes, vainly calling to his friend Malchus, vainly calling to John, the saintly shepherd, vainly calling to the green-eyed dog Qitmir, vainly calling to the Lord his God: the darkness was as thick as tar, the silence – the silence of the tomb of eternity. All he could hear was the dripping of water from invisible vaults, the grinding of eternity in the clepsydra of time.

Oh, who can divide dream from reality, day from night, night from dawn, memory from illusion?

Who can draw a sharp line between sleep and death?

Who, O Lord, can draw a sharp dividing line between present, past, and future?

Who, O Lord, can separate the joy of love from the sadness of memory?

Happy are they who hope, O Lord, for their hopes shall be fulfilled.

Happy are they who know what is day and what is night, O Lord, for they shall revel in the day and revel in the night and the repose thereof.

Happy are they for whom the past has been, the present is, and the future will be, O Lord, for their lives shall flow like water.

Happy are they who dream by night and recall their dreams by day, O Lord, for they shall rejoice.

Happy are they who know by day where they have been by night, O Lord, for theirs is the day and theirs is the night.

Happy are they who recall not their nocturnal wanderings, O Lord, for theirs shall be the light of day.

20

They lay on their backs in a dark cave on Mount Celius, with their hands crossed in prayer like corpses, all three of them, Dionysius and his friend Malchus and, a short distance away, John, the saintly shepherd, and his dog, Qitmir.

They slept the lifeless sleep of the dead.

Had you come upon them in that condition, you would surely have turned and fled; fear would have turned you to stone.

The Mirror of the Unknown

This story does not begin abruptly, *in medias res*, but gradually, as when night falls in the woods. They are dense oak woods, so dense that a ray of the setting sun breaks through the treetops only here and there, for a moment, at the whim of a fluttering leaf, then drops to the ground like a spot of blood and disappears immediately. The girl does not notice it any more than she notices the day fading, the darkness coming on. She is absorbed in something else: she is following the vertiginous leap of a squirrel whose long tail glides along a tree trunk, swiftly, giving the impression of two animals chasing each other, identical in movement and speed yet different – the first, the real squirrel, is sleek and reddish-brown; the second, following close behind, has longer, lighter-colored fur. They are not (thinks the girl, more or less), they are not twins, they are sisters; they have the same father and the same mother. Just as the three of them – Hanna, Mirjam, and Berta (that is, herself) – are three sisters with the same father and the same mother and look like one another yet are different. Hanna and Mirjam, for example, have black hair, pitch-black, while she, Berta, has red hair, bright red, and braided in such a way that it looks a little like a squirrel's tail. Such are the girl's thoughts as she wades through the moist leaves and evening falls on the woods. Then, as in a dream, she comes upon several long-stemmed mushrooms, a whole patch of long-stemmed mushrooms, and she knows for certain, though no one has ever told her, that they are poisonous: it's obvious from their nasty appearance. (The girl is not mistaken, the girl is right: they are poisonous mushrooms, *Ithyphallus impudicus*, which she does not, should not know.) She tramples them with her patent-leather shoes, pulverizing them in a fit of anger. And her shoes, look at them, they aren't even muddy: she walks through the leaves as on a carpet; all you can see is a thin film over the shiny leather surface, the film that forms on an apple or a mirror when you breathe on it. Which reminds her of the mirror her father bought her from a Gypsy at the Szeged fair, and she takes it out of her pocket. (The Gypsy, a young man who was lame in one leg and had a mustache and a mouth full of gold teeth, was selling copper kettles. It was the only mirror he had. He had begged the gentleman to buy it, 'out of kindness.' He would give it to him cheap: he hadn't sold anything the whole day and his baby was ill, dying. . . 'Gypsy business.')

The girl brings the mirror up to her face, but for a moment she does not see anything. Just for a moment.

The country road that leads westward all the way to Makó (and then, turning slightly to the northeast, as far as Budapest) is easily passable at this time of year: the floods have yet to begin, the Maros has yet to overflow its banks. The road begins on the outskirts of Arad. The paved section comes to an abrupt end at the brick factory, and the dirt road is dusty in summer and full of puddles and mud, if not completely flooded, in autumn. But a simple rainfall can turn the dust into a thick yellow mud that sticks to wheels and spokes, and horse hooves sink deep into the doughy clay. Even light gigs and stewards' black coaches leave deep tracks in the mud, not to mention heavy, handmade carriages pulled by two massive, ponderous dray horses.

On the open front seat sits a gentleman in his forties, a man with large black eyes and heavy, drooping eyelids and a slightly threadbare, stiff-brimmed hat on his head. He holds the reins loosely, like an experienced coachman, both straps in one large, kid-gloved hand. In the other hand he clutches a whip, brand-new, elegant, with a copper-faced bamboo handle and a long, thin, leather plait which, on the far side of a small red pompom, turns into a good, solid lash with a viper-like hiss.

The whip's owner had cracked it only once, on his way out of Arad, at the spot where the paved road turns to dirt. Or, to be more exact, twice: the first time in front of the shop, into the void, a trial run, like a customer trying out a hunting rifle, nestling it on his shoulder, inclining his head, closing his left eye, aiming at the cuckoo that has just jumped out of the clock, crying 'Bang-bang,' removing it from his shoulder, opening it, peering down the barrels, examining the carved butt (a deer that has come to a sudden standstill), weighing it in his hands, while the cuckoo disappears behind double doors painted with red roses and green leaves, disappears as if blasted to pieces by the buckshot bursting from the two barrels almost simultaneously (bang-bang), because the hunter has hit it as it was about to take shelter behind its rambler-rose doors, having barely had time to chirp three times – the hands showed three on the dot, the shop of the Arad merchant Rosenberg had only just opened, and our customer, or potential customer, was the first to enter the shop this afternoon.

So he laid down the gun (rather reluctantly, we feel) and picked up a whip standing in a corner together with five or six of its kind, all made of bamboo and identical in length and price, squeezed the handle with both his powerful hands and gave it a twist. The dry bamboo creaked, but gave nicely. Then he lashed it against his boot legs once or twice, but even that was not enough, so he went out in front of the shop, into the street, and swung the whip over his head as veteran cowherders do. The whip hissed like a viper – at which point its fortunate owner abruptly switched direction and gave the handle the kind of tug a fisherman gives a bamboo rod when a large sturgeon or perch takes the bait or that a driver gives the reins when faced with sudden danger, when out of the woods into the path of his cart jumps a bear or two highwaymen, one grabbing the horse by the halter, the other sticking a shotgun in the driver's chest and snatching the reins out of his hands – and a shot, as powerful as a rifle shot or nearly so, rang out along the empty street, which reverberated with the crack.

The second and last time the satisfied customer used his whip was when he left the paved stretch outside Arad and drove into the rutted dirt. Here it had its first true trial, not into the void. He waved it once and only once above the heads of his horses (Waldemar and Christina by name) and cracked it in the air just above their ears. The horses jerked out of their lethargy and, heavy and lumbering though they were, raced through the mud, to the great joy of the two girls in the back seat of the carriage, who, holding on to each other and squealing as if frightened, enjoyed it all greatly, the whole wild ride.

The gentleman is wearing (and may the spanking-new whip not cause us to lose sight of it) a suit of English tweed, with an overcoat, also tweed, but differing in pattern. He gives the impression, an impression that may be false, of being quite satisfied, despite obvious fatigue, and not just because of the whip he has purchased (which is only a trifle) but also, doubtless, because of the mission he has successfully completed. For (kind sir) it is no easy task to enroll one's daughters in a school for children from what people refer to as 'the best families.' Yes, he would never have succeeded without certain connections, plus a tidy little sum, a small gift, actually. . . But, thank Jehovah, the mission has been accomplished. Hanna and Mirjam – the older fourteen, the younger thirteen – would live with a woman in Arad by the name of Goldberg, a woman so strict and moral that she had never married, though, to tell the truth, she was neither so poor nor, shall we say, so *unattractive* as to rule out the possibility of some honest Jew making her happy.

Such are the thoughts most likely occupying Mr Brenner (for that is his name) as he jolts along on the seat of his imitation tilbury each time the wheels hit a mound of dirt. Szeged is still a long way off, two or three hours at least, but he is in no hurry. He has not used the whip again even once or pulled in the reins. The horses know the way, having often drawn the tilbury (let us agree to call it thus) from Arad to Szeged and back: Mr Brenner takes it on business at least once a month to Arad (and to Makó, Temesvár, Kecskemét, Szabadka, Újvidék, Szolnok, and even Budapest). So he abandons the tilbury to his horses' instincts and himself to his thoughts. What a Central European Jewish merchant thinks about on the day of his death we can only guess. Just as we can have only the vaguest idea of what the daughters (thirteen and fourteen) of a Central European Jewish merchant think or dream of on the day they have been enrolled in a secondary school and had their first encounter with the great outside world. The world to come.

That they did not care for the Goldberg woman, a distant relative on their mother's side, was beyond any doubt. Not merely because her upper lip was covered with down (Hanna had whispered 'A mustache!' into her sister's ear) but also because she lost no time in showing how strict she was.

Mindlessly strict, too. At lunch that day she'd made them 'mop up' the lentils left on their plates with a piece of bread! And the constant advice. You'd think they were still children. Do this, don't do that. This is *hoch*, that is not. So much for their mother's stories about what a fine woman Mrs Goldberg or, to be precise, Miss Goldberg was! If she was such a 'fine woman' (Hanna whispered into her sister's ear), why hadn't she married, why hadn't she found herself a husband to 'mop up' the *sólet* on his plate? Mirjam assented, silently, by shutting and immediately opening her eyes: it was all too true – Miss Goldberg was a boring old maid! Really! As for the school. . . Well, the teacher was pretty, young, and nice enough, and she was wearing a hat you'd never see in Szeged – with a ribbon *and* a feather – and a dress she could only have ordered from Budapest, if not Vienna; as for the school itself, however, they had to admit they were somewhat disappointed. True, the outside was just as it should be: large, yellow, newly roofed, and surrounded on all sides by a garden, but inside. . . ! The desks (they had been shown their own classroom), the desks were just like the ones at the Szeged school, an inch or two higher, perhaps, hard to tell, but the same dark color, dark green, and just as scuffed and stained with spots and scrawlings – names, doodles, formulas – that could not be erased. The blackboard was the same too, more black than dark green (as it had been originally), and full of scratches; the red lines that had once formed squares were hardly visible and then only at the edges. The teacher's desk was protected by a sheet of ordinary blue wrapping paper tacked to the top. The high windows were covered with bars, like monastery windows in novels. And this was the Girls' High School!

Gone the squeals of delight when they had set off that very morning before dawn, the joy that fills a child's heart at moments that mark the great turning points in life. All that remains is a secret sorrow, which each keeps to herself. Each is ashamed to confess to the other that she is disappointed, brutally, irreparably, after days and days of joy and exhilaration and after that morning, when they had felt their hearts full to bursting with excitement: *the big day* had arrived!

Sitting there under the hood, wrapped in a warm blanket, they make believe they are drowsing, but each is absorbed in her own thoughts. The oak branches rustle in the wind. Now and then they open their eyes, secretly, and gaze up past their father's shoulders at the arch of leaves through which they are passing as through a tunnel. From time to time the wind drops a leaf on their leather seat. The leaf alights with a barely perceptible scratch, like a mouse.

What could they tell their mother? Surely they are thinking of that as well. How to conceal their sudden drop in spirits? How to keep from disappointing her, their mother, who had seen them off that morning with tears in her eyes as if sending them off to their nuptial bed or, heaven forbid, to death. . . No, no! They couldn't tell their mother that they had been disappointed by the blackboard, that they had been disappointed by the desks. It would be childish, it would hurt her. But Miss Goldberg, that was another story! Would they have to go through a whole year of school 'mopping' their plates clean with their bread? What was the point of it? Granted, the room suited them to a T, the bed was larger, the sheets starched, the eiderdown soft and warm, and the window faced a flower garden with a lilac bush – everything was as nice as could be, but couldn't their dear, kind mother write her a letter and ask her nicely, politely, to stop teaching them 'manners'? Granted, there was a vase full of freshly cut irises on the table in their room, the curtains were as stiff as cardboard, as white as snow, everything was perfect, the bathroom was done in pink earthenware tile and the towels monogrammed *H* for Hanna and

M for Mirjam, but. . . No, they couldn't tell Mother, because after everything they had been through, after six months of long talks, at night, before bed, about going to Arad, to the school, it would be sacrilegious and childish to show how insensitive and ungrateful they were.

It is still light out, though the sun has begun to set. Only Mr Brenner can see it from his throne of a seat, and he may be reminded of a line of poetry – Mr Brenner is a poetry lover, trade has not completely robbed him of a sense of beauty – a line of poetry about the setting sun, which falls beneath the horizon like the blood-bathed head of a monarch rolling off the block.

Lost in thought, Mr Brenner takes a cigar from his inside pocket.

At that moment, at that very moment, the girl in the woods takes the small round mirror in the mother-of-pearl frame out of her pocket and brings it up to her face. First she sees her freckled nose, then her eyes and red, squirrel-tail hair. And then her face disappears, slowly, gradually – first the freckles on her nose, then the nose itself, then the eyes. Her breath spreads across the mirror like a thin film across a green apple. But she continues to hold the mirror in front of her face, because now she sees the woods and the swaying oak leaves. A bird flies up out of a bush, suddenly but noiselessly; a tiny butterfly, the color of rust and faded leaves, vanishes against the trunk of an oak; a deer comes to a sudden standstill, as if stunned, only to dart off again an instant later; a dead branch falls from a tree; a spider's web with a drop of dew refracting a blood-red sunbeam begins to quiver. A pinecone has fallen silently, a branch snapped without a sound, as if made of ashes.

The girl looks into the mirror, bringing it all the way up to her eyes as if she were nearsighted (like Hanna, who wears glasses). Then she sees just behind her or, rather, behind the mirror – because there is nothing behind her, no road – the dusty road and a tilbury riding past. Her father is sitting in the front seat. He has just taken a cigar from his pocket and, laying his whip in his lap, brings a lit match up to it. Now he tosses away the match, which describes a high arc before falling to the ground. All at once he gives the reins a tug. There is terror in his eyes. . . Two men have leaped into the tilbury.

The girl screams out in her sleep, then sits up in bed, clenching in her sweaty hand the little mother-of-pearl mirror, which she has been guarding under the pillow. Mrs Brenner, who has let the child sleep in the room with her that night (usually the three girls sleep in the nursery next door), awakes with a start and, still half asleep, gropes for a candle. The girl is wailing like someone gone mad. It is the cry of an animal, inhuman, a cry that makes the blood run cold. Overturning the candlestick, Mrs Brenner rushes to the child and clasps her to her breast, but she cannot say a word, her voice refuses to function, she does not know what is happening: has someone tried to strangle the girl or slit her throat? Then from the wailing and disjointed cries she makes out something indistinct and horrible; she hears the names of her daughters and a terrifying 'No! No! No-o-o!'

At last she finds the candlestick near the bedside table and, with hands that scarcely obey her, lights a match. The girl is still wailing, wild-eyed, staring into the mirror she clutches in her hand. Mrs Brenner tries to take it from her, but the girl holds on to it with all her might, with the grip of rigor mortis. Mrs Brenner sits down on the bed, holding the flickering candle above her head. In the dim light of the flame she sees – for a moment, only for a moment – the wild eyes of her youngest daughter (if they are not her own wild eyes). Then she rushes over to the wardrobe. A tinkle of crystal rings out. Then the noise of broken glass.

Mrs Brenner goes back to the bed, holding a tiny bottle. Vinegar, eau de Cologne, or smelling salts. The girl is sitting up, her body racked with convulsions, her eyes staring into the void. Next to her, on the floor, lies the broken mirror. The girl looks up at her mother as if seeing her for the first time in her life.

'They are all dead,' she says in a voice almost not her own.

Marton Benedek, the local mayor, lights a candle on his bedside table and glances at the clock: it is after eleven. The dog in the courtyard is barking furiously; he can hear it straining at the chain, and the chain gliding along a taut wire. Someone is knocking at the door, banging his fists, hard. Mr Benedek slips into his dressing gown and goes out without taking off his pom-pommed nightcap, which has slipped down over one ear. Holding up the candle at the door, he recognizes Mrs Brenner clutching her youngest daughter in her arms. The child is shuddering with stifled sobs. When Mrs Brenner cannot manage to get out a word, the mayor reluctantly shows her into the entrance hall.

The dog continues to wail, producing an awful animal plaint closer to an old man's weeping than to the mewling of a child. Mrs Brenner – deathly pale and still clasping the child, whose animal-like whimper proceeds unabated – does her best, dazed as she is, to explain to the mayor the reason for her visit.

'You can see for yourself the state she's in,' she says all but inaudibly.

'Yes, I can,' says the mayor, 'but I'm sorry, I don't quite understand.'

At that point the child turns and looks at him in a way he has never seen before.

'They are all dead,' says the girl, and starts sobbing again, her body twitching with convulsions.

Mr Benedek glances over at the child's mother questioningly.

'She says she saw them in the mirror. They've all been killed, she says. You can see for yourself the state she's in.'

'The mirror?' the mayor asks.

A long explanation follows. Mr Benedek, a man of great experience (fifteen years' worth, if not twenty), does not believe in miracles; he puts his trust in science. The girl, he thinks to himself, has had an attack of hysterics or epilepsy (but he does not say so). All he says is that she should be taken to the doctor first thing in the morning; she may be constipated. And now – it's getting close to midnight – they'd best go home; everything will be all right. The child has had a little *cauchemar* (he uses the French word, apparently to make his hypothesis sound more convincing, like a medical diagnosis pronounced in Latin); what she needs is some Epsom salts (take them, please, keep the whole bottle), but surely, Mrs Brenner, you don't expect me to go traipsing through the woods with my men to confirm the nightmares of a child, a child not even *seriously ill* but merely feverish. Has she ever had mumps? She has? What about whooping cough? There, you see? Maybe it's whooping cough. The first symptom. Agitation, overstimulation of the organism. Exhaustion. And when the body suffers, the soul. . . Whereupon Mr Benedek launched into his theory of the interconnection between spiritual and corporal phenomena, which theory he had doubtless heard at cards from Dr Weiss. Unless he had read it in a book somewhere. Or in the *Aradi Napló*. (Have no fear. Everything will be all right.)

*

For the end of our story we must refer to the 1858 run of the same *Aradi Napló*, which Mr Benedek doubtless read daily, as did Mr Brenner for that matter, to keep up with local marriage announcements, deaths, forest fires, and crimes, as well as with the price of timber, leather, and grain. (Besides official news, the paper carried pastoral letters, educational articles on agriculture, legal advice, and reports on horse races in Budapest, uprisings in Greece, and palace coups in Serbia.) In an issue dating from early in the reign of Franz Josef we find the testimony of Mayor Benedek himself, sworn testimony all the more valuable in that it comes from a man who, by his own account, was free of superstition and inclined to 'positivism.'

'It was a terrible sight' (Mr Benedek's words as quoted by the *Aradi Napló*). 'Out of consideration for the reader we shall refrain from describing the pitiable state in which the victims were found. Mr Brenner had been literally *decapitated* with a knife or ax, while his daughters. . .' There follows a discreet allusion to the fact that the girls had also been slain, and only after the two men had had their way with them.

Locating the perpetrators of the loathsome crime (if we may summarize the *Aradi Napló* account) was not difficult, because the girl had had a clear look at them in the mirror. The first was a twenty-eight-year-old shop assistant by the name of Fuchs, the second an unemployed laborer named Mészáros. Both had worked the previous year for Mr Brenner. They were found in Fuchs's shop with a bundle of bloodstained banknotes. 'Confronted with the evidence, they admitted their guilt. They added that they recognized the hand of God in the speedy discovery of the crime and asked for a priest to hear their confession.'

Other European newspapers reported the unusual incident to their readers, sometimes expressing an unhealthy skepticism, the result of the ever-increasing inroads made by positivism in progressive bourgeois circles. Spiritualist publications – and their influence was considerable – cited it as a sure sign of human magnetic powers. A similar point was made by the celebrated Kardec, an undisputed authority on the subject and a man known to have allied himself with the powers of darkness.

The Story of the Master and the Disciple

What follows took place at the end of the last century in Prague, 'city of mysteries.' The event – if it can be called such – has been described, with negligible variations and modifications, by many authors, and I shall keep to the version provided by Chaim Frankel – the advantage of his narrative residing in the fact that it recapitulates the views of other disciples who have written about the Master. Once we have set aside its heavy-handed disquisitions on faith, morality, Hasidism, disquisitions interspersed with frequent quotations from the Talmud and Frankel's own quibblings, the story comes down to this:

The learned Ben Haas (born Oskar Leib) began to write poetry, in Hebrew, at the age of fourteen. In about 1890 he returned from a pilgrimage to the Holy Land and settled in Prague, where he gathered a group of like-minded scholars around the journal *Ha-Yom*, which was reproduced by hand in as many copies as there were disciples. Ben Haas taught morals and literature. His teachings, set forth in numerous papers and articles and published in part only recently (thanks to the same Chaim Frankel), rest on a moral dilemma that stems from Plato and may be summarized thus: art and morality are based on two divergent premises and as such are incompatible. One might even claim, with Frankel, that all Ben Haas's oeuvre, poetic as well as philosophical, represents an attempt to overcome this contradiction. He attempts to soften Kierkegaard's 'either/or', even though the examples he takes from the history of ideas – from that of literature, primarily – show the dilemma to be virtually insurmountable. 'Art is the work of vanity, morality the absence of vanity', he repeats at several points, as he interprets the lives of great men from King David to Judah ha-Levi and Solomon Ibn Gabirol. The circle headed by Ben Haas (some say it had five members, others seven) set itself the goal of refuting the dilemma by word and deed; that is, of submitting 'in the very heart of poetic temptation' to a rigorous code of morals which, as Frankel points out, was based on the Judaeo-Christian tradition, Talmudic postulates, Kant, Spinoza, and Kierkegaard, yet was not devoid of certain 'anarchistic elements'. If we have understood Frankel correctly, however, the 'rigorous moral imperative' (as Ben Haas called it) did not exclude certain hedonistic principles from its code: contrary to all expectation, vodka, Indian hemp, and the pleasures of the flesh occupied the same rank as reading, travel, and pilgrimages. All Frankel sees here – and I feel he comes close to the truth – is the low point in the intersection of art and morality, where these forces clash in their most elemental form, 'beyond good and evil': the true moral dilemma begins and ends with the issue of vanity; all else lies beyond the moral sphere. The parallels Frankel draws with Buddhist doctrine and bonze practice – in which the pleasures of the flesh raise no barrier to the absolute known as the *tao* – would seem to be a consequence more of private speculation on the part of Ben Haas than of the direct influence of Oriental wisdom. The fact that Ben Haas was seen in a disreputable district of Prague at the age of thirty (by which time he had established his moral code once and for all) cannot, therefore, be considered a scandalous contradiction of the principles set forth in his *Summer and the*

Desert. 'Art is cognition, and cognition is sexless,' Frankel cites as one of Haas's basic postulates. 'Sexless, that is, immoral.' In other words, the learned Ben Haas, who combined in himself the poet and the moralist, two contradictory vocations, strove to reconcile sexless cognition through art, to which all experience is precious, with those ethical principles that would not impoverish it: 'If one takes a person at his word, though it be the Sacred Word, one risks a moral fall graver yet than if one breaks a commandment prescribed by that Word.' This brief quotation from the early Haas contains the simplest explanation of one of the fundamental ideas that years later would spawn the heavy, convoluted, barely comprehensible philosophical doctrine he expounded in Kabbalistic jargon weighed down with neologisms and a number of concepts whose meaning escapes us. Yet we cannot quite agree with Frankel when he states that the obscurity of Ben Haas's later teachings is merely the consequence of doubt, the fruit of 'maturity.' (There are many obstacles in the way of issuing a critical edition of Ben Haas's complete works, the first being the presence of certain rabbis and moralists on the committee charged with their study and publication.)

Although the events that interest us here and that we shall briefly relate have no direct connection with Ben Haas's philosophical doctrine, they do derive, however insignificant they may seem, from the essence of his teachings and call into question an entire complex system of values. Making a sort of moral, if you like.

In the year 1892, and in that same disreputable district of Prague, Ben Haas, who was by then known as the Master, met a young man who asked to speak with him. The Master, torn between the ethical and the poetic principles (the former telling him to refuse, the second to consent), sits down with him in a squalid tavern and orders two glasses of paschal vodka, which was apparently part of the ritual. Yeshua Krochal, for such was the young man's name, confides to the Master that he has begun to frequent this district since he came across one of his writings and read about experience being 'sexless, that is, immoral', but that he has been unable to find the spiritual equilibrium preached in *Summer and the Desert*. The Master is overcome with anguish and remorse when he realizes that his teachings, like every doctrine founded on morality, are liable to cause as much harm as good in immature hands. (For, as Plato observes, a master chooses his disciple, but a book does not choose its reader.) Carried away by an infernal impulse and probably by the vodka (if it was not merely an unconscious wish to parody Pygmalion, as Frankel has it), Ben Haas decides to turn an insignificant creature – the disciple has not answered a single of the Master's veiled questions – into a Hasid (in the sense of one who is 'initiated', 'learned', 'meek'). The young man confesses that *Summer and the Desert* has given him the moral strength to frequent brothels, maintaining that this was primarily an 'act of experience', though he is aware that the 'act of experience' has no value unless it serves a creative function. Ben Haas abruptly sets his vodka glass on the table when Yeshua Krochal pronounces the name of the book he is writing: *The Road to Canaan*. Over the course of the evening, however, the man called the Master grows convinced that his future disciple has all the traits which, had he listened to the voice of reason, would have dissuaded him from taking him under his wing, for stupidity combined with ambition is more dangerous than any kind of madness. He nonetheless arranges for them to meet at the same tavern in three months' time and leaves, after dictating a list of twenty-seven books devoted to the miracle at Canaan and salvation.

At the end of August, Yeshua Krochal appears at the appointed place with his *Road to Canaan*, a manuscript of approximately one hundred and twenty pages, over which the Master casts a fleeting, *all-encompassing* glance, notes the penmanship and picks out several spelling errors at random. He then schedules another meeting, again in three months' time and at the tavern, and sends Yeshua away with another list of books, including a handbook of Hebrew orthography.

On the occasion of their third encounter, in February 1893, the Master leafs through the manuscript with his divining-rod fingers and perceives, to his horror, that his suspicions were well founded: the spelling error on page 72 has been corrected, but the manuscript is otherwise untouched. Driven by a sudden feeling of contrition and, possibly, sympathy (because he has realized or at least sensed that by his example he has transformed an unfortunate citizen into a more unfortunate Hasid and that there is no way out, no turning back), the Master picks up the manuscript and leaves. He spends all that night poring over *The Road to Canaan*, whose futility and emptiness remind him of his own error: had he, on that night nine months before, followed his ethical principle instead of his poetic one (though who can tell where the exact border between them lies!), he would not now have on his conscience a futile human existence that he was obliged, by moral law, to save from the abyss on whose brink it stood. And had that once healthy young man not been infected by his teachings, no matter how misinterpreted or misunderstood, he would not have sat up at night over a senseless text written in a large, careful hand, a text pervaded only by a vain desire to justify the meaninglessness of existence – or the premonition of its meaninglessness – by a creative act of some kind. In a flash of illumination, Ben Haas apprehends that his own vanity has led to this pass, his poetic eccentricity and his passion for polemics; in sum, the urge to prove to his disciples that the story of Pygmalion lacks the moral force of myth and is merely a scandalous anecdote on which the illusion of myth has been conferred.

So as not to reject *The Road to Canaan* in its entirety and abandon the unfortunate Yeshua Krochal in a dangerous wilderness at the age of thirty-three (Frankel rightly discerns in the cryptography the influence of Kabbalistic symbolism on Ben Haas), the man called the Master purges the manuscript of everything in the image of its author, in the image of his vanity: the only trait holding his frail being together. He liberates the manuscript from those ephemera that reflect, as in a puddle, Yeshua Krochal's pockmarked face, the blue circles under his eyes and his lethargic body; with a nimble pen he rids the manuscript of malicious allusions to contemporary events and of biblical digressions, such as the one about Lot's wife, in whom he recognizes a redheaded German woman from the Korona Tavern. (The only mysterious links between the red-headed German woman and Lot's wife were the large white sweat stains around her armpits and the fact that Yeshua Krochal had, by his own testimony, 'sodomized' her.)

Of the hundred and twenty pages in *The Road to Canaan*, barely a third remain, linking those parts in which a hint of mythic allegory seems to lurk, a hint that might be turned into the Appearance of Substance. The next day, bleary-eyed and ill-tempered, Ben Haas sets off for the Korona with the manuscript of *The Road to Canaan* in the pocket of his caftan. He finds Yeshua Krochal in dejection. The young man tells him of his doubts: he has come to realize the *futility* and the *inevitability* of his choice. If the Master thinks that *The Road to Canaan* cannot attain the grace of form, nothing will be left but for him to *withdraw*. He utters the last word in a highly ambiguous manner, lending it a different and more pernicious meaning than the one it had in *Summer and the Desert* ('If you are unable to act at the perilous conjunction of these contradictory forces, the moral and the poetic, then withdraw. Water the cabbages in your garden, and grow roses only in the cemetery. For roses are fatal to the soul'). The man called the Master then takes the thickly annotated manuscript from the inside pocket of his silk caftan and lays it in front of the young man.

'If I understand correctly,' says Yeshua, dejected, 'there is nothing left.'

'On the contrary,' says Ben Haas. 'What is left is what can be given the Appearance of Substance. And the difference between the Appearance of Substance and Substance is so imperceptible that only the wisest can detect it. As the wise are very few – only thirty-six in the whole world, according to some – very few will notice it. For the vast majority, Appearance equals Substance.'

Yeshua Krochal's face lights up, because he thinks he has detected his own secret idea in the Master's words, his guiding idea: that all things here below happen under false pretenses, on the thin and elusive border separating Substance and the Appearance of Substance, but since no one is able to ascertain what is one and what the other (here his idea differed fundamentally from the Master's), all values, ethical and poetic, are merely a matter of skill and chance – empty form. Ben Haas senses his disciple's hidden idea – for the man called the Master did distinguish Truth from Falsehood – and determines to show him the boundary between essence and illusion. He takes him home and, in the course of the night, seeks to explain, with simple yet instructive examples, how an idea, the shadow of an idea, or a single image can lead – by the magic of the word and the enchantment of what remains unexpressed – to the grace of form.

At dawn Yeshua Krochal leaves the Master's room (in which the strong odor of leather-bound books was leavened by the intoxicating fragrance of sandalwood blasphemously burning in brass menorahs: souvenirs from the Master's pilgrimages). He stops at the Korona and orders goulash and a tankard of beer, then sets to copying out the manuscript. By noon the complete text of the biblical parable entitled *The Road to Canaan* lay on the table before him, a clean copy in his own large script. Then he takes the manuscript containing the Master's emendations and tosses it into the great tile stove like a cathedral, with doors to heaven and hell. When the flame has destroyed all trace of the Master's hand and thereby, as if on a pyre, of his own soul, Yeshua Krochal folds his manuscript, slips it into the inner pocket of his coat, and, burning with a fever till then unnoticed, orders another tankard of beer. As Karolina sets the beer down on the edge of the table, Yeshua leaps up and grabs one of her large round breasts. Karolina stands stock-still for a moment, *like Lot's wife transformed into a pillar of salt*, then starts and swings her arm. Her heavy red hand grazes his nose.

'This is the Appearance of Substance,' says Yeshua sententiously, 'while that' – he cups his hand and spreads his fingers wide – 'was Substance.'

The Road to Canaan appeared at the end of 1894, first in the journal *Ha-Yom* in Hebrew, then, early the next year, translated into German, as a book. The book earned the universal acclaim of the exegetes, all of whom found that it had, as Frankel says, 'Substance.' Only young Bialik (later known as Chaim Nachman), who subjected the work to a serious analysis, discovered traces of the Master's hand, which 'tries to save the parable from the void of which it reeks.' Bialik's criticism had the following consequences: in the afterword to the new edition of *The Road to Canaan*, Krochal proclaimed that Bialik was a syphilitic and publicly renounced Ben Haas's teachings, calling him a charlatan and a 'poisoner of souls.' True to his position, he allied himself with the Master's adversaries and, in a new publication called *Kadima*, led a long and merciless battle against him, 'using gossip and slander in a manner that showed him to be not entirely without talent.' One unfinished parable found among Ben Haas's papers, entitled 'The Story of the Master and the Disciple,' contains no moral, being incomplete. Except perhaps the following: It is difficult to establish a clear-cut difference, in the moral sense, between Substance and the Appearance of Substance. 'Not even the man called the Master always succeeded in doing so,' says Frankel. 'Leaning over the abyss, not even he could resist the vain pleasure of trying to fill it with Sense.' Whence we may draw a new lesson, which suggests, in proverbial style, that it is dangerous to lean over someone else's void even in the vain desire to find one's own reflection there, as at the bottom of a well: for that, too, is vanity. Vanity of vanities.

Pro Patria Mori

When, at dawn on that April day, the day set by Imperial decree for his execution, the guards entered his cell, the young Esterházy was kneeling on the floor, his hands tightly clasped in prayer. His head was bent low and his light hair fell to either side, revealing a long, thin neck and bony spine that disappeared under a collarless linen shirt. The guards paused, considering a count's conversation with God sufficient reason to disregard, for a moment, the strict rules of Spanish ritual. The priest also shrank back, mutely clenching the hands he had brought together in prayer. His palms were sweaty and had left a telltale stain on the ivory covers of the breviary; his rosary, its beads the size of olives, swung silently. The only sound came from an enormous ring of keys which was held by one of the guards and clanked two or three times, unrhythmically.

'Amen,' the young man whispered, coming to the end of his morning prayer. Then he added, out loud, 'Forgive me, Father.'

At that moment, as if by command, the drums began to beat, as sinister and monotonous as rain.

A ruddy-faced, bushy-mustachioed hussar officer framed by the long rifles of two Croatian uhlans, one on each side, started reading out the sentence. His voice was hoarse, and the empty cell resounded. The sentence was harsh and inexorable: death by hanging. The young nobleman, weapon in hand, had taken part in one of the mass uprisings – sudden and unforeseen, bloody, brutal, and hopeless – that shook the Empire from time to time only to be just as suddenly, brutally, and hopelessly crushed. His descent and the renown of his family had been treated by the court as aggravating circumstances, as a betrayal not only of the monarch but also of his own class. The punishment was meant to set an example.

The condemned man could make out scarcely a word among the string of monotonous syllables throbbing in his ears like drumbeats. Time had stopped. Past, present, and future had merged, the drums beat on, and his temples, like a frantic pulse, pounded with the far-off sounds of victorious assaults and battles, triumphal processions, and with the beating of other drums, drums draped in black, no longer announcing *his* death but the death of another. His youth notwithstanding (he looked more like a boy too tall for his age than like a mature young man), he had seen blood flow and come face to face with death, though never yet at such close range. And the very proximity of death, the sensation of it breathing on his bare neck, distorted the view of reality reaching his consciousness, just as for an astigmatic the proximity of an object serves only to make it appear more misshapen. All that mattered to him – because what his world valued most besides an honorable life was an honorable death – was to preserve the dignity required of an Esterházy at such a moment.

He had spent the night awake but with his eyes shut and without so much as a single audible sigh, so that the guard, whose eye was glued to the peephole, might testify that the condemned man had slept soundly, as if he were going to the altar rather than to his death. And, in a strange inversion of time, he could *already* hear the guard telling the officers' mess, 'Gentlemen, the young Esterházy slept quite soundly that night, without so much as a sigh, as if going to his wedding rather than to his hanging. I give you my word as an officer!

Gentlemen, let us render him his due!' After which is heard –
he hears – the crystal ping of glasses. 'Chin chin!'

This ecstasy of death, this victorious self-control did not
leave him all morning. He maintained his composure through
prayer, gritting his teeth to resist the cowardly behavior of his
intestines and solar plexus, those traitors to will and deter-
mination; he tempered his manhood with the legend of his
family. Thus it was that when, in accordance with compas-
sionate protocol, he was vouchsafed a last request, he did not
ask for a glass of water, though his insides were on fire; he
asked for a cigarette, like an ancestor who had once, long
before, requested a pinch of tobacco, which he had then
chewed and spat in the face of his executioner.

The officer clicked his heels and offered him his silver cigarette case. ('Gentlemen, I give you my word as an officer. His
hand did not tremble any more than mine trembles now as I
hold this glass. Chin chin!') In the rays of the early-morning
sun, which cut diagonally across the cell as across the cells of
saints in old paintings, the cigarette smoke rose violet like the
dawn. The condemned man sensed that the smoke, a resplen-
dent illusion, had momentarily sapped his strength, broken
him, as if he had heard the far-off sound of a taragot spilling
across the plain, and he quickly tossed the cigarette to the
floor and crushed it with a spurless hussar boot.

'Gentlemen, I am ready.'

Chosen for its military starkness, as brief as a command, as
bare as an unsheathed saber, and as cold, the phrase was meant
to be pronounced like a password, without emotion, as one
says 'Good night, gentlemen' after a spree. But now he felt it
did not sound at all worthy of history. His voice was pure and
sonorous, the syllables distinct, the sentence straightforward
but somehow flaccid and a little broken.

Since the day his mother visited him he had realized that despite a wild hope, wild and secret, his life was henceforth no more than a tragic farce written by people nearly as powerful as gods.

She had stood before him, stolid, strong, with a veil over her face, filling the cell with her personality, her persona, her character, her large plumed hat and her skirts, which rustled though she made not the slightest movement. She refused the simple prison stool proffered by the uhlans, according her an honor they had surely never accorded anyone else in this place; she pretended not to notice them placing the simple wooden seat, frightfully simple beside her silk flounces, next to her. She thus remained standing throughout her visit. She spoke to him in French, so as to bother the hussar officer stationed off to one side at an appropriate distance, his sword across the left shoulder in what was more an honor guard's salute to the aristocrat (whose nobility was as ancient as that of the Emperor himself) than a precaution or threat to the proud woman visiting the Imperial casemate.

'I shall throw myself at his feet,' she whispered.

'I am ready to die, Mother,' he said.

She cut him off sternly, perhaps too sternly, *'Mon fils, reprenez courage!'*

Then for the first time she turned her head slightly in the direction of the guard. Her voice, still no more than a whisper, fused with the whisper of the flounces. 'I shall be standing on the balcony,' she said, all but inaudibly. 'If I am in white, it means that I have succeeded in . . .'

'Otherwise, you will be in black, I presume,' he said.

He was wrenched from his lethargy by the drums, which had started beating again, nearer now it seemed, and he realized, from the sudden animation of a scene which had theretofore stood immobile before him in a kind of mute permanence, that the reading of the sentence was over: the officer rolled up the scroll; the priest leaned over him and blessed him with the sign of the cross; the guards took hold of his arms. He did not allow the two uhlans to lift him, but rose lightly to his feet, barely supported. Then, even before he had crossed the threshold of the cell, he experienced a sudden feeling of certainty – appearing first in his breast, then suffusing his entire body – that it would all end as the logic of life demanded. Because everything was now arrayed against death, everything in this nightmare stood on the side of life: his youth, his origins, his family's eminence, his mother's love, the Emperor's mercy, and the very sun streaming down on him as he stepped into the carriage, his arms bound behind his back as if he were a common criminal.

But that lasted only for a moment, only until the carriage reached the boulevard, where a boisterous mob, gathered from all over the Empire, stood waiting for him. Through the intermittent drumrolls he heard the buzz of the crowd, its threatening murmur; he saw fists raised in hate. The crowd was cheering Imperial justice, because the mob always cheers the victor. That realization crushed him. His head sank a bit on his chest, his shoulders drew slightly together as if warding off blows (a stone or two was hurled), his back bent a little more. But the difference was enough for the rabble to sense that his courage had left him and his pride was shattered; it elicited cheers of something akin to jubilation. (Because the mob loves to see the proud and the brave brought low.)

When he came to the head of the boulevard, where the residences of the nobility began and the crowd thinned out a bit, he raised his eyes. In the light of the morning sun he glimpsed a blinding white spot on the balcony. Leaning over the railing, all in white, stood his mother, and behind her – as if to enhance the lily-white brilliance of her dress – the enormous dark green leaves of a philodendron. (He knew that dress well: it was an heirloom; one of his ancestors had worn it to an Imperial wedding.)

Immediately, almost insolently, he straightened up, wishing to make it clear to the threatening mob that an Esterházy could not die just like that, could not be hanged like some highwayman.

And thus he stood beneath the gallows. Even as the hangman removed the stool from under his feet, he awaited the miracle. Then his body twisted at the end of the rope and his eyes bulged out of their sockets, as if he had just seen something awful and terrifying.

'I stood only a few paces away from him, gentlemen,' the hussar with the bushy mustache told his fellow officers at mess that evening. 'When the rope went down over his neck, he watched the hangman's hands as calmly as if they were tying a brocade scarf for him . . . Gentlemen, I give you my word as an officer!'

There are two possible conclusions. Either the young aristocrat bravely and nobly, in full awareness that death was certain, his head held high, or the whole thing was merely a carefully staged performance with a proud mother pulling the strings. The first, heroic, version was upheld and promulgated – orally, and then in writing, in their chronicles – by the *sans-culottes* and Jacobins; the second, according to which the young man hoped to the very end for some magical sleight of hand, was recorded by the official historians of the powerful Habsburg dynasty to prevent the birth of a legend. History is written by the victors. Traditions are woven by the people. Writers fantasize. Only death is certain.

The Book of Kings and Fools

1

The crime, not to be perpetrated until some forty years later, was prefigured in a Petersburg newspaper in August 1906. The articles appeared serially and were signed by the paper's editor-in-chief, a certain Krushevan, A. P. Krushevan, who, as the instigator of the Kishinev pogroms, had some fifty murders on his conscience. (Throughout the darkened rooms, mutilated bodies lie in pools of blood and raped girls stare wild-eyed into the void from behind heavy, rent curtains. The scene is real enough, as real as the corpses; the only artificial element in the nightmarish setting is the snow. *'Pieces of furniture, broken mirrors and lamps, linen, clothing, mattresses, and slashed quilts are strewn about the streets. The roads are deep in snow: eiderdown feathers everywhere, even covering the trees.'*) Thus, Krushevan would take credit for being the first to publish a document demonstrating the existence of a worldwide conspiracy against Christianity, the Tsar, and the status quo. He did not, however, disclose the *origin* of the mysterious document – on which he based his indictment – making do with an offhand remark to the effect that the text was written 'somewhere in France.' The title given to it by the anonymous translator was *The Conspiracy, or The Roots of the Disintegration of European Society*.

Krushevan submits an expanded version of *The Conspiracy* to the Imperial censors, and it appears as a book one year later, under the patronage of the Imperial Guard. The publisher is the Petersburg Society for the Deaf and Dumb. (It is difficult to judge whether this name is somehow symbolic.)

Krushevan's texts, the cause of many passions and much puzzlement, eventually fell upon fertile ground and found a ready ear in the person of an eccentric hermit who, while awaiting signs from heaven in his Tsarskoe Selo solitude, was engaged in preparing an account of his personal mystical revelations. Father Sergei Nilus, as he was called, considers *The Conspiracy* a confirmation of his own suspicions and evidence of the disintegration of faith and practice. He therefore includes the precious document in his *Antichrist*, treating it as an integral part of a revelation that has enlightened two souls simultaneously. And as proof that the heavenly hosts were not yet vanquished.

The local Red Cross chapter volunteers to publish Nilus's book. It is printed as a deluxe, gold-embossed, Japanese-paper edition to remind the reader of human artistry, which can be a refuge from evil and a source of new, platonic stirrings. One copy was reserved for His Imperial Majesty Nicholas II. (The Tsar fairly devoured mystical works, believing that hell could be avoided by a combination of education and skill.) Those who had the privilege of being initiated into the Great Mystery revealed by the book were thunderstruck: the workings of European history, more or less from the French Revolution on, were laid out before them. Everything that had previously seemed the result of chance and heavenly machination, a battle of sublime principles and fate, all of it – this murky history as capricious as the gods on Olympus – was now clear as day: someone here below was pulling the strings. Here was proof not only that the Antichrist exists (which no one had doubted) but also that the Evil One has his earthly acolytes. The Metropolitan of All the Russias, who felt the scales fall from his eyes as he pictured the legions of the Antichrist invading Holy Russia, commands all his three hundred and eight Moscow churches to read out excerpts from the book instead of celebrating Mass.

Thus the stern laws of the Bible, which preach justice and severe punishment, are now supplemented by the mysterious *Conspiracy*. For *The Conspiracy* contains, or appears to contain, everything that is in the Scriptures: laws and penalties for transgressors. Its origins are almost as mysterious as the origins of the Bible, with its modest compiler, Nilus, appearing merely as commentator and editor; a sort of exegete. The only difference is that *The Conspiracy*, despite its murky origins, remains a human creation, which makes it seductive, dubious, and criminal.

We shall now try to investigate the origins of this text, glancing briefly at those who created it (endowing my insolent procedure with the prerogatives of divine anonymity), and, finally, pointing out the evils that followed from it.

2

Sergei Alexandrovich Nilus, author of *The Antichrist*, Father Sergei to initiates, enters the historical arena direct from the dark ages of Russian feudalism. Having lost his estate, he makes pilgrimages to monasteries, where he lights long yellow candles for the repose of sinful souls and beats his forehead on the cold stone of the cells. Wherever he goes, he studies the lives of saints and holy fools, and discovers in them analogies to his own spiritual life. This leads him to the idea of writing down the story of his own wanderings – from anarchism and godlessness to the true faith – and proclaiming his revelation to the world: contemporary civilization is perishing; the Antichrist is at the gates, already burning his shameful brand in hidden places – under women's breasts and on men's groins.

Krushevan's articles appear just as Nilus was completing his autobiography. 'The seed fell upon fertile ground.'

In May 1921 a French traveler by the name of du Chayla published an article (in the belief that the Revolution had wiped the old sinner from the face of the earth) treating Nilus with the respect customarily reserved for the dead: 'Before opening the precious chest, he read me fragments from his book and from the source material he had gathered: the dreams of Metropolitan Philaret, an encyclical of Pope Pius X, the prophesies of St Seraphim of Sarov, together with passages from Ibsen, Solovyov, Merezhkovsky . . . Then he opened the reliquary. Lying there in frightful disarray were detachable collars, silver spoons, badges of various technical schools, monograms of the Empress Alexandra Fyodorovna, a cross of the Legion of Honor. His febrile imagination discerned the "seal of the Antichrist" – a triangle, or two crossed triangles – in everything: galoshes manufactured in Riga at the Treugolnik (Triangle) Factory, the Empress's stylized initials, the five arms comprising the cross of the Legion of Honor.'

Monsieur du Chayla, reared on the Enlightenment, looks upon all this with doubt and suspicion, demanding *proof positive*. The 'Charter of the Reign of the Antichrist' is clearly a hoax, no less than Edouard Drumont or Léo Taxil's, which recently duped the whole of the Catholic world. While the doubting disciple of positivism sets out his suspicions, Father Sergei suddenly stands and snuffs out the candle with his bare fingers. The sun had set, but the room was still light: the snow shone white outdoors and the samovar glistened like a Chinese lantern. Nilus beckons his visitor over to the window. The silhouette of a man on his way to the monastery stood out against the snow. They could hear the snow crunching beneath his feet. 'Do you know who that was?' Father Sergei asked after the footsteps have died away, his eyes gleaming with a maniacal gleam. 'The pharmacist David Kozelsk, or Kozelsky. (With them, one never knows.) On the pretext of seeking a shortcut to the ferry – which is on the far side of the monastery grounds – he is snooping about, trying to get hold of *this*.' And he covers the book, lying in its black slipcase on his desk, with his huge peasant fist. Even in the semi-darkness the visitor could make out a small gilt image of the Archangel Michael on the front. Father Sergei makes the sign of the cross over it as if blessing a loaf of bread.

3

Maria Dmitrievna Kashkina, née the Countess Buturlina, has this to say about Father Sergei from a distance of thirty years: 'Nilus lived with his wife, née Ozerova, and his first mistress, a divorcée, in a house belonging to the monastery. A third woman, sickly and always accompanied by her twelve-year-old daughter, would join them from time to time. Nilus was rumored to be the girl's father. (The girl served as medium at the séances arranged by Nilus's friends.) I often saw them out walking together – Nilus in the middle, sporting a long white beard, a bright peasant shirt, and the rope of a monk's habit around his waist; the two women on either side, hanging on his every word; and the girl and her mother tagging along behind. When they reached the woods, they would stop in the shade of a tree; Ozcrova would take out her watercolors, the other woman her knitting, and Nilus would stretch out next to them and gaze up at the sky in utter silence.'

In the following passage, the same M. D. Kashkina lifts a corner of the veil concealing the crazed world in which *The Conspiracy* found fertile soil, a world combining superstition, deranged mysticism, and the occult with religious fanaticism and debauchery: 'Nilus had befriended a monk at the monastery, a man of rather questionable morals but not without talent as a painter. On Nilus's suggestion, the monk had done a painting showing the Imperial family hovering in the clouds while horned devils emerging from dark cumuli brandish pitchforks and stick out their forked tongues menacingly at the young Tsarevich. The devils are held at bay by a local monk, Mitya Kalaida, also known as Barefoot Mitya, who has come running to crush the Satanic hosts and save the Tsarevich. Nilus, thanks to his wife, née Ozerova, contrived to have the canvas presented to the court in St Petersburg. Mitya was quickly sent for. He arrived attended by Nilus, who translated the incomprehensible mutterings of the feebleminded monk into human speech.'

4

A biography of Nilus published in Novi Sad in 1936 depicts Sergei Alexandrovich as a man of God, a righteous man, and accepts the mysterious *Conspiracy* document as an authentic channel, much like the mouth of a medium, for the voice of the Devil. Prince N. D. Zhevakhov (who came to Novi Sad via Constantinople and found there a countryside similar to the countryside of his childhood: a plain gently rising into hills like a wave of green) does not doubt for a moment the arguments set forth in *The Conspiracy*: it is 'the work of an infidel and dictated by the Evil One himself, who revealed to him his scheme for destroying the Christian nations and achieving world domination.' (As for Prince Zhevakhov, I have a feeling I met him once on a cold day in 1965 in a Novi Sad cafeteria near the Catholic churchyard. He was a tall, thin, slightly stooped man with a pince-nez and a dark threadbare jacket and greasy black tie; in other words, he fit his contemporaries' description of him. He spoke with a heavy Russian accent and sported the Order of St Nicholas on his lapel. He stood at a counter, leafing through the filo pastry of a baklava with slender nicotine-stained fingers as if it were a book.

From Zhevakhov's biography we learn, to our surprise, that Sergei Alexandrovich Nilus spent the years immediately following the Revolution in peace and quiet somewhere in the south of Russia with his wife, née Ozerova. (All trace of the other two women was lost in the turmoil of the Revolution, but there is some indication that the twelve-year-old medium became a police informer.) Nilus shared his rooms with a hermit by the name of Seraphim and gave sermons in a nearby chapel. The terror, the famine, the blood – they were all so much evidence that the reign of the Antichrist would come about exactly as *The Conspiracy* had predicted. The triangles, which had previously assumed the guise of a mysterious code, now swarm about openly – like beetles – engraved on the buttons of military tunics and caps. (At this point Father Sergei scoops a handful of metal buttons from the deep pockets of his mantle and holds them out as a *corpus diabolici*.)

From a letter – postmarked Oran, Marseilles, Constantinople, Paris, Sremska Mitrovica, and Novi Sad; it reached Prince Zhevakhov like a message from the other world – we learn that in the terrible year of 1921 a three-man Red Army detachment happened upon the house in which the two righteous men were living and that the soldiers were about to kill them when a monk appeared in their path, his arms raised to heaven. The soldier in charge, a well-known local bandit, triangles gleaming like fresh wounds on the cap above his forehead, is suddenly convulsed and topples from his horse as if struck by lightning. The horse swings around and bolts, followed by the other bandits. When Seraphim the hermit and Father Sergei turned to thank the mysterious guardian monk for saving their lives, all they found on the spot where he had stood a moment before, raising his arms to heaven, was a hovering wisp of mist and a patch of trampled grass, already uncoiling like green springs.

The ultimate victory, however, fell to the Evil One. Late one night a unit from the NKVD knocked on the door of the monastic residence. Their torches showed Father Sergei huddled against his wife on one side and the stove, still warm, on the other. Grabbing him by the beard, they pulled him out of bed. The righteous protector who had saved them the first time failed to reappear. Sergei Alexandrovich Nilus died of a heart attack in a labor camp on New Year's Day 1930, never knowing that he had with his *Antichrist* prepared a crime that would soon take place. (His wife, Ozerova, a former lady-in-waiting at the court, ended her days seven years later in a labor camp on the Arctic coast.)

5

While Father Sergei, far from the madding crowd, collects tokens of the Devil, a copy of his book falls into the hands of the former Empress, then spending the days of her captivity at the Ipatiev house in Yekaterinburg. A crack squadron of White cavalry eventually manages to take the town, but arrives too late: all that was left of the Imperial family was a heap of bones. Here is how a contemporary, Bykov by name, describes the event: 'At about two o'clock in the morning confused gunfire breaks out in the cellar of the Ipatiev house. We hear terrified cries for help, then a few isolated shots finishing off one of the children. And then the heavy silence of the Siberian night. The corpses, still warm, are transported in utter secrecy to a nearby wood, where they are hacked to pieces, doused with sulfuric acid, doused with gasoline, and set on fire. The awful mixture of putrid, mashed human remains and charred bits of bone and jewelry – gleaming diamonds on purulent flesh – was hastily tossed into an abandoned mine.'

The commission set up in the Ipatiev house to compile an inventory of the possessions left by the Imperial family (Tula samovars with ivory handles, tapestries, French porcelain chamber pots, several eighteenth-century masters, and one unsigned canvas in which the Imperial family, their eyes gouged out, are drifting toward heaven on a bank of clouds) discovers the Empress's personal library under a heap of furniture and valuable icons. The books are for the most part ecclesiastical or mystical texts in German, French, and Russian. Three of them definitely belonged to the Empress: a Russian Bible, the first volume of *War and Peace*, and Nilus's *Conspiracy* (the third edition, of 1917). On each of these books the Empress, anticipating her ineluctable end, had drawn a swastika, symbol of happiness and God's grace.

6

The chance discovery of *The Conspiracy* with the swastika drawn by the blessed hand of the Empress had the force of revelation for many. According to the testimony of English officers attached to Denikin's army, there was a popular edition for 'all soldiers able to read,' and it was meant not only to bolster the men's tottering morale but to commemorate the holy martyr, Alexander Feodorovna.

Gathering round the fire, the soldiers listen to their officers reading from Nilus's prophesies and *The Conspiracy*, the silence between words interrupted only by the whisper of large snowflakes and the occasional neigh of a Cossack horse at what sounds like a great distance. 'If every state has two enemies,' the crystal-clear voice of the officer rings out, 'and if the state is permitted to all possible force against a foreign enemy – such as night raids, for example, or offensives with vastly superior numbers – why should it consider such measures impermissible and unnatural against the worst enemy of all, the one who would destroy the existing social order and prosperity?'

The officer lowers the book to his side for a moment, marking the place with his index finger. 'That, gentlemen, is the kind of morals *they* preach.'

(The officer's orderly takes advantage of the break to brush away the snow that has collected on the tent flap over his head.)

'The word "freedom"' – enunciating the word as if it were in italics – 'incites human societies to do battle with every force, every power, even the divine. Which is why, when *we* rule the world. . .' (Here again he lowers the book, his finger between two pages.) 'I don't imagine I need tell you, gentlemen, who the mysterious "we" are; *we* are *they.*' He then raises the book, satisfied that this formulation has made the point for him. 'And so when *we* – that is, *they* – have conquered the world, we shall consider it our duty to expunge the word "freedom" from the vocabulary of man. For freedom is the incarnation of the life spirit and has the power to turn the crowd into bloodthirsty beasts, though, of course, like all beasts, once given their fill of blood, they fall asleep and are then easily enchained.'

Armed with their new knowledge, the rabid troops embark on pogroms with a pure heart. A certain *Encyclopedia* – whose objectivity has been contested by some, especially *Conspiracy* addicts – estimates the number of persons massacred between 1918 and 1920 to be approximately sixty thousand, in the Ukraine alone.

7

The luggage of White officers (departing their homeland on Allied ships) was wont to include – among the New Testament and Dahl's *Dictionary* and monogrammed towels – a copy of *The Antichrist* complete with fingernail markings in the margins. The almost immediate French, German, and English translations of the book were greatly facilitated by the Russian émigrés' linguistic prowess.

Experts have been hard put to clear up the mystery of the manuscript's origin. Their learned commentaries, teeming with muddled and contradictory statements, lead one to conclude, *tout compte fait*, that access to the text on which *The Conspiracy* is based involves great danger. The archive housing the original is a kind of antechamber to hell – one does not enter twice the gate sealed with seven seals of mystery. Indeed, only one person has ever succeeded in entering even once, a person combining the cunning of a fox, the agility of a cat, and the heart of an otter. French sources claim that a woman stole the manuscript in Alsace (or Nice) while her lover slept the sleep of the just, never suspecting that his secret dream of world conquest would soon be proclaimed to a blind and deaf mankind. According to a statement by Pyotr Petrovich

Stepanov, former procurator of the Moscow Synod, former Court Counselor, and so on and so forth, a statement made under oath on the 17th of April in the year 1927 at Stari Futog, the said Stepanov had the manuscript in his possession as late as the turn of the century. He published it in a Russian version at his own expense, with no indication of year or place of publication, no reference to author or publisher – 'for personal use only.' The manuscript had been delivered to him from Paris by a woman friend. A Madame Shishmaryova identifies the author as a follower of Maimonides by the name of Asher Ginzberg: the original Hebrew text set down in his hand somewhere in Odessa serves, she claims, as the basis for all ensuing translations. The plan for world conquest, born in the sick mind of Maimonides's disciple, was supposedly approved by his cohorts at a secret congress in Brussels in 1897. Russian émigrés were known to favor prominent supporters with a typed copy of *The Antichrist* in translation (incorporating *The Conspiracy*), and at a Paris masked ball in 1923 *The Antichrist* – together with a roast goose and a tin of caviar – was the prize for a winning raffle ticket. And that unfortunate exile, Joachim Albrecht of Prussia, passed out copies of the Nilus book to waiters, taxi drivers, and lift boys! 'All the gentlemen need do is read it through and everything will be clear – not only the reasons for my own exile but also the causes of the unprecedented rate of inflation and the scandalous deterioration in hotel services.' A copy of the book bearing the Gothic-script signature of the last Hohenzollern (it was inscribed to the head chef of a leading Parisian restaurant, though his unworthy heir later put it up for auction) indicates that the Prince owned the first German edition, which was printed in 1920, at the instigation of the same German nationalist elite that published the notorious *Auf Vorposten*. 'No book since the invention of the printing press, since the invention of the alphabet, has done more to fan the flames of nationalist fervor,' the journal reported in a telling overstatement. Its conclusion is apocalyptic: 'If the nations of Europe fail to rise up against the common enemy who reveals its secret plans in this book, our civilization will be destroyed by the same ferment and decay which destroyed classical antiquity two thousand years ago.'

Five reprintings in quick succession testify to the work's indubitable popularity.

Its authenticity is also beyond doubt: Nilus's *Antichrist*, the basis for all translations, exists in black-and-white at the British Museum. And since most mortals look upon any printed word as Holy Writ, many have accepted the book itself as proof and think no more about it. 'Can it be that a band of criminals has actually worked out such a plan,' asks a horrified *Times* editor, 'and is even now rejoicing as it comes to life?' The collection housing the prima facie evidence harbors many secrets among its dust-laden shelves. When chance, fate, and time meet in a favorable constellation, their point of intersection will of necessity pass through the dusky vaults of the British Museum.

8

One strand of our intricate narrative now takes us to a third-rate hotel off a large square. In the foreground we see a religious edifice – a cathedral or a mosque. Judging by the faded green stamps on the postcard, it could be Hagia Sophia. The card is postmarked 1921. A Russian émigré is living in the hotel; he is Arkady Ippolitovich Belogortsev, a cavalry captain in wartime, in civilian life a forestry engineer. We know very little about his past; he does not like to speak about it. (His letters deal with the weather, God, and customs of the Orient.) The services he once performed for the Tsarist secret police, the Okhrana, have lost their luster here in exile. The main reason he left Russia, he claims, is that he feels an obligation to uphold his allegiance to the Tsar: an officer may not break his oath. This categorical imperative – a Prussian–Junkerish conception of honor – led him, on an English ship, to Constantinople. Here he dropped anchor. Filthy hotels, cockroaches, nostalgia. A. I. Belogortsev found it more and more difficult to hold his head up. First he pawned a silver watch with the Tsar's initials and a gold chain (a gift from his father); then he sold his copy of Dahl's *Dictionary of the Russian Language* (after removing his *ex libris*: two crossed swords with a cross in the middle), his ceremonial saber, the silver snuffbox, the signet ring, the kid gloves, the amber cigarette holder, and finally, his galoshes.

One fine day it was time to sell all the other books in his cherry-colored suitcase. (In their terrible leisure the White officers used poetry as a kind of spiritual hygiene, a substitute for political passions. The works of the Russian poets went round and round the secondhand bookshops like cards passing from hand to hand.) Belogortsev's only consolation came from a bit of ad hoc wisdom: by the time one has reached maturity, one has derived all there is to be derived from books – illusion and doubt. One cannot forever cart one's library around on one's back like a snail. A man's personal library is only what stays in his memory – the quintessence, the sediment. (To him the name Dahl sounded like the title of a poem.) And what was the quintessence? He knew *Onegin* by heart, *Ruslan and Ludmila* nearly by heart; he recited Lermontov while applying alum to his shaving nicks ('*S svintsom v grudi. . .*'), and sometimes Blok, Annensky, Gumilyov, the odd fragmentary line or two from others. And what was the sediment? Some stanzas by Fet, Byron, Musset. (Hunger, *pace* the Stoics, is no help to memory.) Verlaine, 'Le Colloque sentimental,' Lamartine, and various other bits and pieces that surfaced at random, out of context: '*Vous mourûtes au bord où vous fûtes laissée*,' by Racine or Corneille.

'Besides, gentlemen, what is the point of having a personal library? At best, it is no more than an *aide-mémoire*. Let us set aside poetry for the moment,' the former owner of the family library continues, 'and turn to *serious matters*. (Perhaps the Bolsheviks are right when they claim that poetry is mist or propaganda.) We are in the woods, somewhere in Anatolia or Serbia. (Apropos, everyone is heading for Serbia now.) Here with me is our dear' – he goes up to her, takes her by the hand; they go for a stroll through the woods – 'Yekaterina Alexeevna. . . Moonlight. I am who I am, as Hermes Trismegistus would say, that is, Arkady Ippolitovich Belogortsev, a forestry engineer in civilian life. (That is very important, gentlemen: *a forestry engineer*.) All at once Yekaterina Alexeevna asks the fatal question: "Tell me, please, what kind of flower is that?" I am an honest man and cannot dissemble. "Dear et cetera, et cetera, I must confess I don't know. But," I add instantly, "I can run home and look it up in my *handy* reference library."'

They all laugh. Yet they also realize that the only reason Arkady Ippolitovich is talking like this, albeit in his cups, is to vent his grief at having sold the library which he has hauled over land and sea in a leather suitcase, on his back, like a snail.

Mr X, the lucky buyer, who 'kept a certain distance' from it all, feels uneasy. He has the impression that all eyes are on him and that they are full of reproach.

9

The next day, though a little hung over, X looks through the books; for he has not examined them properly yet. The reports of their value – excluding sentimental value, of course – now appear overblown. The only work in the lot he finds worthy of interest is *Field Notes of a Russian Officer*, which he would return to Arkady Ippolitovich if that would not seem insulting. He had purchased the books *en bloc*, as he later said, and principally to prevent 'the moral collapse of a Tsarist officer and friend.' There is no denying, however, that he grew interested, sincerely interested, in the *Field Notes* (with Lazhechnikov's autograph) as he sat hunched over the leather suitcase in his wretched room at the Royal (not the Royal in the center of town, the other one, the one that wears its battered signboard like a sneer). 'And what will remain of us, gentlemen?' he said then and there in an undertone, as if to himself. 'Love letters!' Whereupon his companion blurted out, 'And unpaid hotel bills.'

The list is not particularly long. De Las Cases, *Mémorial de Sainte-Hélène* (no date; the front matter has apparently been torn out); *Selected Sketches and Anecdotes of His Highness the Emperor Alexander I*, Moscow, 1826; *Letters of M. A. Volkova to Madame Lanska*, Moscow, 1874; P. M. Bykov, *The Last Days of Tsardom*, London (no date); *The Confessions of Napoleon Bonaparte to the Abbot Maury*, translated from the French, Moscow, 1859; I. P. Skobalyov, *Gifts for Friends, or Correspondence of Russian Officers*, St Petersburg, 1833; Marmont, *Mémoires 1772–1841*, Paris, 1857 (the first three volumes, with the autograph 'Marmont, maréchal, duc de Raguse'); Denis Davydov, *Materials for a History of Modern War* (no date or place of publication); Mistress Braddon (Mary Elizabeth

Braddon), *Aurora Floyd*, St Petersburg, 1870; Count F. V. Rastopchin, *Notes*, Moscow, 1889; D. S. Merezhkovsky, *Tolstoy and Dostoevsky*, St Petersburg, 1903 (signed and inscribed to a certain V. M. Shchukina); A. S. Pushkin, *Works*, edited by V. I. Saitov in three volumes, Imperial Academy of Sciences, St Petersburg, 1911; Knut Hamsun, *Complete Works* (the first four volumes), St Petersburg, 1910; *Materials on the History of the Pogrom in Russia*, Petrograd, 1919; A. S. Pushkin, *Correspondence 1815–1837*, St Petersburg, 1906; L. N. Tolstoy, *War and Peace*, third edition, Moscow, 1873; L. N. Tolstoy, *Sevastopol Sketches*, Moscow, 1913; Richard Wilton, *The Last Days of the Romanovs*, London, 1920; *A Survey of Notes, Diaries, Memoirs, Letters, and Travelogues Bearing on the History of Russia and Published in Russia*, three volumes, Novgorod, 1912; Elie de Cyon, *Contemporary Russia*, Moscow, 1892; Jehan-Préval, *Anarchie et nihilisme*, Paris, 1892 (there is reason to believe that the man behind this pseudonym is a certain R. Ya. Rachkovsky); William Makepeace Thackeray, *Vanity Fair: A Novel without a Hero*, Tauchnitz edition, Leipzig (no date); N. I. Grech, *Notes about My Life*, published by Alexei Surovin, St Petersburg (no date); Eugène-Melchior de Vogüé, *Les Grands Maîtres de la littérature russe* (volumes 55, 56, and 64), Paris, 1884; *Field Notes of a Russian Officer*, published by Ivan Lazhechnikov, Moscow, 1836; *Transactions of the Free Economic Society for the Development of Agriculture in Russia*, St Petersburg, 1814; *Letters of N. V. Gogol*, in Shenrok's edition, Moscow (no date); D. I. Zavalishin, *Notes of a Decembrist*, St Petersburg, 1906 (inscribed by the author to Ippolit Nikolaevich Belogortsev); and finally a cheaply bound book with no title page.

(The reader will, I trust, easily identify which books in the list form part of the family patrimony – the books bound in leather – and which are more recent acquisitions and therefore likely to afford some insight into the intellectual profile of their owner, a former Okhrana officer about whom little is otherwise known.)

10

After leafing through all the books – not without curiosity and a kind of metaphysical trepidation ('What will remain of us, gentlemen? Love letters.' 'And unpaid hotel bills') – X puts them back in the suitcase, which smelled of new boots and lavender, and then picks up the book without a title page. (I imagine him crouching by the suitcase, holding the book up to the lamp.) For a while he turned it this way and that. Then he brought it up to his nose. (He loved the smell of old books.) On the book's spine he discovered a word printed in tiny letters. At first he took it for the title of a novel. On page 9 he came across an idea of Machiavelli's – or an idea attributed to Machiavelli – that roused his curiosity: '*States have two sorts of enemies: internal and external. What arms do they use when at war against foreign enemies? Do the generals of two warring states exchange plans of action so as to enable the enemy to put up stout resistance? Do they refrain from night raids, from ruses and ambushes and battles launched with numerically superior troops? And you refuse to make use of their tricks, traps, and snares, their indispensable wartime strategies, you refuse to make use of them against the internal enemy, the disrupters of law and order?*'

At this moment X sees swirls of snow. His mind has wandered far from the hotel room.

'*The principle of national sovereignty*' – his curiosity was growing – '*destroys all semblance of order; it legitimizes a society's right to revolution and thrusts it into open war against*

power, against God Himself. The principle of national sovereignty is the incarnation of might; it turns the people into a
bloodthirsty beast, which, once it has had its fill of blood, falls
sound asleep and can easily be enchained.'

In the balmy Mediterranean night outside his window X
sees huge snowflakes swirling past; in the quiet Istanbul night
he hears the neighing of Cossack horses. Then he sees an officer lowering a book to his side for a moment, marking the
place with his index finger. ('That, gentlemen, is the kind of
morals *they* preach.') In the break that followed, the officer's
orderly brushes the tent flap with his hand. Mr X feels the
snow sliding into the sleeve of his greatcoat. His hangover was
suddenly gone. The scene seemed remote, as if it had happened in the far-off past: huddled together by the fire in a
godforsaken Transcarpathian valley, the men had listened to
their officer read to them about a perfidious conspiracy against
Russia, the Tsar, and the established order of things. The officer in question was an artillery colonel by the name of Sergei
Nikolaevich Dragomirov. The book from which he read that
day to his men had now, after Dragomirov's glorious end (at
the siege of Yekaterinburg), made its way back to X.

Suddenly suspicious, X searches for the book Sergei
Nikolaevich Dragomirov had left him in his will. It was (as the
reader will have guessed) Nilus's *Antichrist*. Dragomirov
believed in that book as he believed in Holy Writ. (X had spent
a good many nights with him – may he rest in peace – talking
about Russia, God, revolution, about death, about women,
about horses and artillery.) Though it had been lugged around
in knapsacks, read and reread, the book retained something of
its original deluxe-edition splendor. Its yellowed pages bore
traces of the nail marks and fingerprints of its former owner –
most likely the only earthly traces left of him.

X compares the two books. At the very beginning of the

anonymous work he discovers a passage that again seemed somehow familiar: '*What serves to bridle those beasts who devour one another and who are called men?*' he read. '*At the dawn of the social order it is crude, untrammeled might; later it is law. But law is merely might regulated by juridical formulae. Might always precedes right.*'

In the other book, Nilus's *Antichrist*, an appendix entitled 'The Conspiracy' contains the following nail-marked passage (he could almost hear the late Dragomirov's sonorous voice): '*What has bridled those bloodthirsty beasts called men? What has guided them even to the present day? At the dawn of the social order, they lived by crude, mindless might; later they submitted to law, which is also might, though masked. I therefore conclude that, according to the law of nature, right resides in might.*' ('That, gentlemen, is the kind of morals *they* preach.')

Despite his innate modesty, which Graves, too, acknowledges, I submit that X (the degrading initial is merely a sign of extreme discretion) was aware of the true significance of his discovery. In the book of unknown authorship he had discovered the secret source of *The Conspiracy*, which for two decades had inflamed minds and sown seeds of suspicion, hatred, and death, but, more important, he had removed the terrible threat hanging over the people whom the book designates as conspirators. (At this point the wild look of a young girl somewhere in Odessa flashed before his eyes. Her head rested on a wardrobe door torn from its hinges – she had tried to hide in the wardrobe – and she lay there stone-like, though still breathing. In the mirror – as in a quotation – one could see mutilated bodies, scattered pieces of furniture, broken mirrors, samovars, and lamps, linen, clothing, mattresses, slashed quilts. The road was deep in snow: eiderdown feathers everywhere – even the trees were covered with them.) On the other hand – and this was important only for him, for his soul – at last he had final and incontrovertible proof against the theses of Colonel Dragomirov (belated proof, needless to say) and in support of his own doubts as to the existence of a secret international conspiracy. 'Besides the Bolshevist one, which has long since been far from *secret*. . . Incidentally, you are aware that by order of General Denikin I conducted an investigation to ascertain whether Russia was harboring a secret conspiratorial group like the one described by Nilus. Well, gentlemen, the only secret organization we uncovered was an organization whose goal was to return the Romanovs to power!. . . No protests, please. We have official reports on it, with statements by witnesses. . . Yes. Any Romanovs at all. . . One day, gentlemen, I arrived just after the *conspirators* had received their punishment. The scene persists in my memory like an open sore. . . Colonel, if your conspirators look like that girl. . .' – Let him finish! A little tolerance, gentlemen! – '. . . and if that is the price Russia must pay. . .' Shouts of indignation, a distant chorus of raucous male voices interrupts his words and memories. ('It's time to go to sleep, gentlemen. We have a hard day tomorrow. . . Gentlemen, may I point out that it's already getting light.')

By the time X had shut the book, now heavily underlined and full of marginal notes, the sun was coming up. Tired as he was, he could not fall asleep. He waited until ten o'clock and put a call through to Graves, the local correspondent of *The Times*.

11

In August 1921 *The Times* of London – the very paper which less than a year before had wondered how *The Conspiracy* 'could have been so prophetic as to have foretold all this,' and a paper with wisdom enough to contradict itself – published an article by its Constantinople correspondent, Philip Graves. Graves respected the desire of his source to remain anonymous. (Thus, as we have mentioned, one of the chance but nonetheless important figures in the affair will forever be designated as X.) All Graves revealed was the man's social background: Russian Orthodox, constitutional monarchist, anti-Bolshevik, orderly to Dragomirov, artillery colonel. Skipping over the unimportant initial telephone call, Graves summed up for his readers the content of the conversation the two men had in the bar of the Hotel Royal (the one in the center of town), a conversation that lasted from five in the afternoon to ten at night: 'A former officer in the Tsarist secret police, now a refugee in Constantinople, has recently been reduced to selling a collection of rare books. The lot includes a cheaply bound 5½ × 3½ volume in French with no title page. A single word, Joly, is imprinted on its spine, and the preface, or "Simple Avertissement," bears the dateline Geneva, 15 October 1864. Both paper and typeface fit the period in question. The reason we include such details is that we believe they will help in discovering the title of the work . . . Its former owner, the onetime Okhrana officer, does not recall how the book came into his possession; nor did he ever attach particular importance to it. The new owner, X, believes it to be extremely rare. While leafing through it one day, he was struck by the similarity of certain of its passages and a number of formulations in the notorious *Conspiracy*. After comparing the works more extensively, he has come to the conclusion that *The Conspiracy* is largely a paraphrase of the Geneva original.'

12

Two books – Nilus's, which served to recruit hordes of fanatics and exacted the bloodiest of sacrifices, and another, itself a sacrifice, anonymous, one of a kind, an orphan among books – two contradictory products of the human mind, so similar and so different, lay for almost sixty years separated by the Kabbalistic distance (and I tremble as I write the word 'Kabbalistic') of four letters of the alphabet. And whereas the former would leave the long, dark rows of shelves (its poisonous breath mingling with the breath of its readers, its margins bearing the traces of their encounters, of revelations – when a reader discovered in the thought of another the reflection of his own suspicions, his own secret thought), the latter lay covered with dust, a dead, unwanted object, kept there not for its thought or spirit but simply as a *book*, the kind that makes the reader who runs across it wonder whether anyone has ever opened it before him and whether anyone will ever, to the end of time, reach for it again, the kind that falls into a reader's warm hands only by chance, by mistake (either he has jotted down the wrong shelf number or the librarian has misread it), leaving the reader to contemplate the futility of all human effort, including his own: he was looking for something else, poetry or a novel, Roman law or a paper on ichthyology, heaven knows what, but something which at the time at least seemed more lasting, less futile than that dusty book with its musty odor, its yellowed pages more affected by the years of dank air than those of other books because its dust has turned to dry rot, the ashes of oblivion, an urn of dead thought.

Thus muses the errant reader.

When chance, fate, and time meet in a favorable constellation, their point of intersection shall fall on that book and, like a sunbeam, illuminate it 'with a great light' and save it from oblivion.

13

One day two journalists with hats pulled down over their eyes like detectives and a letter from Graves in one pocket pay a visit to the library at the British Museum. They had no trouble whatsoever locating the book they were after, under the author's name: Joly. Thus, the mysterious source of *The Conspiracy* (written in Hebrew, according to Madame Shishmaryova, in the hand of Asher Ginzberg, or according to Prince Zhevakhov, taken down word for word from the Evil One's dictation) had after many long years come to light.

The book, which the 'shameless vultures,' as Delevsky calls them, used for their own vile designs – *A Dialogue in Hell Between Montesquieu and Machiavelli, or Machiavelli's Politics in the Nineteenth Century, Written by a Contemporary* – is doubtless, as Rollin says, one of the best textbooks ever composed for modern dictators or anybody aspiring to be one; while according to Norman Cohn it heralds with merciless lucidity the varieties of twentieth-century totalitarianism. 'But that, after all, is a poor kind of immortality,' he adds.

14

The time it takes for man's earthly remains to return completely to dust (a business that mattered to Flaubert, if one may take him at his word, for purely literary reasons) is calculated differently by different parties, and ranges from fifteen months to forty years. In any case, by the time Graves discovers Maurice Joly's book and resurrects it from the dead, the bones of its author had undergone carbonization and merged with earth and mire: he had been dead almost forty-five years.

Maurice Joly, the son of a municipal councilor and an Italian woman by the name of Florentina Corbara, was admitted to the bar in 1859. In an autobiographical sketch, he gives an account of the *Dialogue*'s origins: 'For a year I contemplated a book that would demonstrate the terrible buffets and blows delivered by the Empire's legislation to all areas under its administration, destroying political freedom on every level. I decided that the French would never read so harsh a text. I therefore sought to pour my study into a mold suitable to our sarcastic turn of mind, which since the coming of the Empire had been forced to conceal its barbs ... Presently I recalled the impression made upon me by a book known only to a small number of cognoscenti, the *Dialogues sur le commerce des blés*, by the Abbot Galiani. It put me in mind of setting up a dialogue between people living or dead on the topic of contemporary politics. One evening, while strolling along the river near the Pont Royal, I had an idea; namely, that Montesquieu could easily be made to personify one of the thoughts I wished to express. But who would be a proper interlocutor for him? The answer came to me in a flash: Machiavelli! Montesquieu would represent the rule of law, while Machiavelli would represent Napoleon III and expatiate upon his heinous politics.'

The *Dialogue aux enfers entre Machiavel et Montesquieu* made its way into France in hay wagons (the peasant smuggler thought the cardboard boxes he was transporting contained contraband tobacco), the intention being that the book be distributed throughout the country by men who despised tyranny. But since men prefer the certainty of servitude to the uncertainty that comes of change, the first man to open the book (apparently a humble post-office employee, an 'active trade unionist' overheard the dialogue in the nether regions, recognized the allusion to the ruler, and flung the book as far as he could, 'with terror and disgust.' Hoping for a promotion, he reported the incident to the police. When the gendarmes opened the boxes of books, the amazed tobacco smuggler swore with absolute indignation that someone would pay for this. According to the inspector of police, not a single copy was missing. As certain medieval associations have given book burning a bad, even barbaric name, the books were taken well outside the town to the banks of the Seine, where they were doused in acid.

Maurice Joly was brought to trial on April 25, 1865. Because of the spring rains and a certain silence on the part of the press, only a few inquisitive souls were in attendance. By order of the court, the book was banned and confiscated and Joly fined two hundred francs (the cost of the acid and labor) and sentenced – 'for incitement to hatred and scorn of the Emperor and His Imperial reign' – to fifteen years in prison. Stigmatized as an anarchist, rejected by his friends, unyielding, yet aware that the world would not be set right by books, he took it upon himself early one July morning in 1877 to put a bullet through his head. 'He deserved a better fate,' says Norman Cohn. 'He had a fine intuition for the forces which, gathering strength after his death, were to produce the political cataclysms of the present century.'

15

Owing to an instance of 'obnoxious manipulation' (in Delevsky's words), a pamphlet aimed against tyranny and the amateur despot Napoleon III became a secret program for world domination: *The Conspiracy*. The cynical forgers, trusting the police report, assumed that the sulfuric acid had destroyed all copies of Joly's book (except for the one they had, heaven knows how, managed to procure). Change a few words, add a pejorative remark or two about Christians, take away the venomously ironic sting of Joly's fantasies (ascribed to Machiavelli in the text) and divorce them from the historical context – and you have the infamous *Conspiracy*.

A comparison of the two texts confirms without a doubt that *The Conspiracy* is a forgery and thus that there is no such thing as a program formulated by a 'mysterious, dark, and dangerous force which holds the key to many a troubling enigma.' *The Times*'s sensational discovery, made public under the headline 'Final Brake on Conspiracy,' should, logically, have put an end to the entire long and harrowing affair, which had corrupted many minds and cost many lives.

The quest for the perpetrators of the criminal act and for the motives that led them to commit it did not begin until some twenty years after the events. By then, most of the participants were dead and Russia was cut off from the world. Nilus (Father Sergei) conducted a careful investigation in monastery archives.*

---

* Nilus sought the diary of a hermit who, according to Zhevakhov, described the afterlife with extraordinary realism: 'The author of the diary does not confine himself to throwing light on events of the distant past and predicting events to come; he also affords his readers a picture of the other world with a realism that goes beyond intuition to personal, God-given revelations. I recall his tale about the young man who, cursed by his mother, was seized by a mysterious power [*nevedomaya sila*] and hurled from earth into the void, where he spent forty days living the life of a spirit, in full accordance with the laws that govern them. The story, which contains so much extraordinary material that all possibility of invention or fantasy must be ruled out, represents yet another piece of evidence in favor of the existence of life after death and of the life of spirits'. (Prince N. D. Zhevakhov, *S. A.*

The search for the sources of *The Conspiracy* constitutes a special chapter in what is a fascinating and complex novel. (The word 'novel' makes its second appearance here, in full awareness of its meaning and weight. Only the principle of economy keeps this tale, which is no more than a parable of evil, from assuming the marvellous dimensions of a novel with a chain of events stretching endlessly across the immense land mass of Europe, to the Urals and beyond, to both Americas, with untold protagonists and millions of corpses, against a terrifying backdrop.) The present chapter might be compressed – like the summaries in magazines that reduce great works to their plotlines – into the following miserably schematic and bare outline:

The Conspiracy, or The Roots of the Disintegration of European Society originated somewhere in France (as Krushevan first claimed) in the last years of the nineteenth century, at the height of the Dreyfus Affair, which divided France into two opposing camps. The text, riddled with typically Slavic errors and stylistic infelicities (and famous for an enormous front-page inkblot, a blot resembling the 'Antichrist's seal of blood'), shows that the author of the forgery was Russian. Burtsev says that, just as all roads lead to Rome, all evidence concerning the origins of the first version of *The Conspiracy* (the one that shamelessly plundered and distorted Joly's book) leads to a certain Rachkovsky – 'the talented and ill-fated Rachkovsky' – chief of the Russian secret police in Paris. This Rachkovsky, Nilus maintains, was a selfless crusader against all earthly Satanic sects and 'did a great deal to trim the claws of Christ's enemies.' A man by the name of Papus, who had the opportunity to make his close acquaintance, portrays

---

Nilus Kratkii ocherk zhizni i deiatelnosti [S. A. Nilus: A Short Sketch of His Life and Work], Novi Sad, 1936).

Rachkovsky in a manner reminiscent of the Symbolists – and not just in his use of capital letters: 'Should you encounter him out in the World, I doubt you would harbor the least suspicion on his account, for his Behavior is in no wise revelatory of his mysterious dealings. He is large, energetic, always smiling, and has a horseshoe beard and lively eyes – more Brilliant Jester than Russian Corinthian. Despite a marked weakness for *les petites Parisiennes*, he is doubtless the most skillful Organizer in all the Ten European Capitals' (*L'Echo de Paris*, November 21, 1901). Baron Taube – who some ten years after the Revolution wrote a book entitled *Russian Politics*, in an attempt to explain, primarily to himself, the why and wherefore of the Empire's downfall and to document the major role played by the secret police – also had the opportunity to make his acquaintance. 'Not even his ingratiating manner and sophisticated way with words – he was like an outsize tomcat that prudently hid its claws – could stifle for more than a moment the basic image I had of him as a man of keen intellect, unbending will, and deep devotion to the interests of Tsarist Russia.'

The biography of this man of unbending will is to some extent typical: shifts from left to right or right to left along the ideological spectrum are now a commonplace of European intellectual life, and proof that there are no constants in the dialectics of human development. In his youth Rachkovsky belongs to secret student groups that read banned books and manifestos in hushed voices and carry on secret conversations and secret love affairs, basking in the light of a vague future 'whose only program was the romanticism of revolution.' With his cap pulled down over his forehead at a jaunty angle, he passes through secret passageways into dark cellars reeking of printer's ink and specializing in *sang de boeuf*-colored pamphlets and false identity papers with the most imaginative of names. It is a life full of traps, dangers, and thrills, when a password obtains overnight shelter for a group of strangers, men with heavy beards and blue-blooded girls with unladylike revolvers in their muffs. During that winter of 1879, one of the heavy-bearded, fiery-eyed men who spent the night there smoking in the dark informed on his fellow plotters, 'after coming to doubt the necessity of planting a bomb in a parish church.' Rachkovsky, who had confided to his indecisive comrade the fact that one of General Drentel's assassins had slept in his bed two nights before, soon found himself in the hands of the Third Section of the Imperial chancellery. The result was a scene worthy of Dostoevsky. The state prosecutor, having sized up the personality of the accused, immediately came up with the following proposition: Mr Rachkovsky could either agree to cooperate with the police ('And, after all, *golubchik ty moi mily*, the police are no less devoted to the cause of Russia than are the revolutionaries') or. . . Rachkovsky did not take long to make up his mind. Forced to choose between exile in Siberia ('Siberia, *ogurchik ty moi*, Siberia is romantic even in Dostoevsky, isn't it, now? But reading about it under a warm quilt, if you don't mind my saying so, makes it seem a bit too tame and, how shall I put it, cozy') and a trip to Paris ('a nice little change of scene, *dushenka moya*'), he chose the latter. As one of his contemporaries has observed, Rachkovsky's eloquence, his 'way with words,' burst forth on that February day in 1879 when he accepted the prosecutor's proposition. 'This was his first forgery, this imitation of the prosecutor, this incredible sham.'

The way stations now speed past as if framed by a train window. Less than four years after his arrest (and one stint in prison by mistake), Rachkovsky becomes assistant to the Petersburg Director of State Security, and the very next year he is named Chief of All Secret Services, with headquarters in

Paris. The network he has spun spreads across the map of Europe in a pattern that at first appears confused but gradually reveals an architectonic perfection: Paris – Geneva – London – Berlin. One branch (carefully traced on the map in his room) stretches beyond the Carpathians to Moscow and Petersburg – 'like an aorta leading to the heart of the matter,' as one nostalgic contemporary noted.

Late in 1890 – thanks to flattery, bribery, espionage, and brains (as well as dinners 'where the champagne flowed like water and the guests chattered like magpies') – Rachkovsky uncovers a secret revolutionary organization that is manufacturing bombs in a locksmith's shop on the outskirts of Paris. The bombs are destined for terrorists in Russia. Rachkovsky, thus, hands over sixty-three would-be assassins to the Third Section for transport to Siberia. More than twenty years passed (by which time the Siberian convicts were dying off one by one) before Burtsev discovered it was all a frame-up: the bombs had been made by Rachkovsky's henchmen, the locksmith's shop registered in the name of one of his French confederates.

It was the golden age of anarchists and nihilists, says Norman Cohn, and homemade bombs were all the rage in both Europe and Russia. Today we know for certain that our 'brilliant jester' Rachkovsky stood behind most of the assassination attempts (the nail-filled bomb thrown into the Chamber of Deputies, no less than the more dangerous explosions in Liège) like a hidden God. Rachkovsky was obsessed with the idea of instilling a spirit of doubt in Europe and thereby bringing it closer to Russia. 'Never satisfied with his job as a security chief, he tried to influence the course of international affairs. The prodigality of his ambitions was matched only by the paucity of his scruples.'

16

With unerring shrewdness, Rachkovsky soon perceived that the effect of bomb throwing was relative: when the murders were senseless or less than clearly motivated, the public shuts its eyes tight, as if frightened by a strong bolt of lightning and determined to forget about it as quickly as possible. Experience taught him that political intrigue can trigger explosions with a greater destructive force than any bomb. People are willing to believe whatever they are told, especially people who appear to be morally unblemished. (The corrupt cannot imagine people different from themselves; they can only imagine people who have succeeded in hiding their true natures.) 'Before you prove a slander false, *dushenka moya*, a lot of water will have flowed under the Seine's bridges.' His biographers maintain that he began writing anonymous letters while a secondary-school student, addressing them to teachers, friends, parents, and himself. Now, in his new capacity, he recalled the harmful effects of that youthful pastime, and having both money and a printing press at his disposal, he takes to publishing the 'confessions' of former revolutionaries – their road to disenchantment – in pamphlet form and replying to the pamphlets himself under a pseudonym. The confusion he thus caused was diabolical.

Once, having just published a pamphlet signed 'P. Ivanov,' Rachkovsky gave a potential collaborator this account of the mechanics of slander and its power: 'While you warm your front, *golubchik*, your backside gets cold. It's like sitting around a campfire: you always have one flank, so to speak, exposed. Now there are two ways to protect yourself (nobody's come up with a third), and both are ineffective: either you keep your mouth shut and assume nobody's going to take the lies about you seriously – even if they are in print – or you get so indignant that you answer back. In the first instance people will say, "He's keeping his mouth shut because he's got nothing to say in his defense," and in the second, "He's defending himself because he feels guilty. He wouldn't take the trouble if his conscience were clear." Slander, *ogurchik moi mily*, spreads like Spanish flu.' (Spanish flu was in vogue at the time.)

17

The forged version of Joly's *Dialogue in Hell*, fabricated in 'Rachkovsky's workshop,' fell with amazing speed into Nilus's hands. 'The meeting of these two minds, these two fanatics, was inevitable,' a contemporary remarked. 'The only difference between them was that Nilus was mad and mystical enough to believe in *The Conspiracy* as he believed in the *Lives of the Saints*.' The manuscript reached him indirectly, via a Madame Y. M. Glinka, who held séances in Paris and spied on Russian terrorists in exile. She later claimed her portion of the fame in a confession to a newspaper reporter, but since she also claimed to maintain ties with the otherworld and be in direct communication with deceased members of the Tsar's family, the reporter was rather skeptical about her allegation. Yet the fact remains that she was the one who delivered a copy to Krushevan, who first published it in his newspaper, whence, as we have seen, it came into Nilus's hands.

The rumors set in motion by this 'masterpiece of slander' spread throughout the world at a velocity known only to malicious hearsay and the French disease, racing from the continent to the British Isles, then on to America, and even, on the return voyage, to the Land of the Rising Sun. Owing to its mysterious origins and the need people have to give history a meaning in our godless world, *The Conspiracy* soon became a kind of bible, teaching that there is a 'mysterious, dark, and dangerous force' lurking behind all history's defeats, a force that holds the fate of the world in its hands, draws on arcane sources of power, triggers wars and riots, revolutions and dictatorships – the 'source of all evil.' The French Revolution, the Panama Canal, the League of Nations, the Treaty of Versailles, the Weimar Republic, the Paris métro – they are all its doing. (By the way, métros are nothing but mineshafts under city walls, a means for blasting European capitals to the skies.) From the treasury of its 'irresponsible and occult organization' comes funding for such adversaries of law and faith as Voltaire, Rousseau, Tolstoy, Wilson, Loubet, Clemenceau, Eduard Sam, and Lev Davidovich Bronstein. Among those who fell prey to its intrigues are Tsar Alexander II, General Selivyorstov, and Archduke Ferdinand. Its members, the executors of its will, include Machiavelli, Marx, Kerensky, B. D. Novsky, and Maurice Joly himself (a pseudonym, an anagram in fact, whose origins are easily decipherable in the name Maurice).*

18

The most complete and best-known edition of *The Conspiracy* is surely the four-volume one that appeared in Paris in the twenties. Monseigneur Junius devoted seven years of work to the project, finishing it at the age of eighty-two. It is the work of a scholar, fanatic, and polyglot who did not hesitate to delve into the Slavic languages, 'exceptionally difficult and of no

---

* Two names in this paragraph are fictional. Eduard Sam is the father in Kiš's autobiographical novels *Garden, Ashes* and *Hourglass*, while the revolutionary B. D. Novsky is commemorated in the title story of *A Tomb for Boris Davidovich*. [Trans.]

great immediate benefit,' as one of his biographers has observed. It brings together everything known on the subject and includes a comparison of the French translation with the Russian, German, and Polish, indeed, of each with all the others, pointing out niggling linguistic differences, a great many slips – *lapsus mentis* and *lapsus calami* – as well as flagrant typographical errors in earlier editions, errors that sometimes alter the sense of the original substantially; it also contains biblical analogies, which unequivocally condemn the scandalous authors of this scandalous book. ('For their hand was not guided by the hand of mercy.')

Nor, it bears stating, were his labors in vain. Every publisher of *The Conspiracy* – and not just in France – every *serious* publisher who was after more than cheap fame or easy money now referred to Monseigneur Junius's four-volume edition on all questions of scholarship. (It is highly probable that A. Tomić made use of Monseigneur Junius's work for his version, which appeared as *The True Foundations* in Split in 1929, as did the anonymous commentator who signed himself Patrioticus and whose translation appeared in Belgrade five years later under the unambiguous title *Undermining Humanity*.)

In Germany, belief in the authenticity of *The Conspiracy* was 'unshakable, solid as a rock,' and the book molded the conscience and patriotic sentiments of several generations. While the social-democratic newspapers hotly denounced the accusations made by the 'obscure' work, the segment of the press that tends to refrain from spreading dangerous rumors opted for the other of the two possible ('equally ineffective') stances: it passed over the whole affair in silence, considering – especially in the wake of *The Times*'s discovery – all further discussion unnecessary. In keeping with Rachkovsky's psychological assessment of the situation, the contradictions inherent in the two stances led a then unknown (as yet unknown) amateur painter to write that the very fact that people persisted in trying to prove the book a forgery was 'proof of its authenticity' (*Mein Kampf*). In the infamous year of 1933, when the amateur painter was already *very well known,* more than thirty editions of *The Conspiracy* appeared, and Der Hammer, its publishers, threw a cocktail party to celebrate the sale of the hundred thousandth copy.

The American translation, based on Nilus's version, reached the half-million mark around 1925, thanks in large part to a mass-circulation newspaper owned by Henry Ford, a man with two lifelong obsessions: the automobile and secret societies. In Latin America the book found immediate and lasting application in fierce intra- and interparty squabbles and became a handbook for fanatics, especially among the German population. The third Portuguese edition (São Paulo, 1937, with a crucifix and a three-headed serpent on the cover) may be taken as standard: its editor follows Monseigneur Junius. The same holds for Preziosi's Italian version of the same year. The editorials provoked by the Hungarian edition (1944), which included the woolly wisdom of a certain László Ernő, were directly responsible for a hunting rifle being fired at the windows of our house. (So, one might say, the *Conspiracy* affair closely concerns me, too.)

19

There are clear indications that *The Conspiracy* not only made a deep impression on the amateur painter who wrote the illustrious *Mein Kampf* but also influenced an anonymous Georgian seminary student who was *yet to be heard from.* In the flickering candlelight of the long snowbound nights of Siberian exile, the words of *The Conspiracy* must have affected him more than the Gospels.

Thus it was that a manual written for the edification of a

Renaissance prince – by way of Joly's philosophical reincarnation and Nilus's distorting mirror – became a manual for contemporary autocrats. Several examples from Nilus, together with their historical reflections, will demonstrate why the text has had so fateful an impact.

'*Men with evil instincts outnumber men with good instincts. Governing by violence and terror therefore yields better results than governing by academic argument. Every man aspires to power, every man would like to be a dictator if he could, yet few men are willing to sacrifice the welfare of all to their own personal welfare.*' – The Conspiracy, p. 216.

Or: '*Our right lies in might. The word "right" is fraught with responsibility, yet its meaning has never been determined. Where does it begin? Where does it end? In a state where power is poorly organized and the ruler weak, sapped by a plethora of liberally inspired laws, I set down a new right – the right of the stronger to attack and rip the existing order and its institutions to pieces.*' – p. 218.*

There remains the complex issue of whether the deed precedes the word or whether it is merely a shadow of the word. A few quotations from *The Conspiracy* might lead us to believe in the idealistic variant. The moral that future tyrants drew from the work has turned into ardent, steadfast practice.

'*Our duty is to spread discord, strife, and animosity throughout Europe and thence to other continents. The benefit will be twofold: first, we shall keep all democratic states at bay by proving we can bring about their downfall or alter their social system at will; second, we shall pull the strings in which we have*

---

* The grandiloquence of this passage attests to the influence exercised by *The Conspiracy* on a certain Dr Destouches, author – as Louis-Ferdinand Céline – of the tract entitled *Bagatelles pour un massacre.*

enmeshed all governments with our politics, economic treaties, and diplomatic obligations.' – p. 235.

Never in the history of ideas has a philosophy intended for a ruler found a more faithful reverberation or fulfilment.

'*Politics has nothing in common with morality. A leader who rules morally is not political and therefore has no business at the head of state . . . From the evil we are constrained to do at present will come the good of an intractable regime, the only regime suited to the essence of nationhood, so sadly undermined in this day and age by liberalism . . . The end justifies the means. Let us therefore set aside the good and moral and concentrate on the necessary and useful.*' – p. 218.

'*We must see to it that no more conspiracies rise against us. We shall therefore punish mercilessly any armed opposition to our power. All attempts to found secret societies of whatever nature will result in the death penalty. We shall disband all societies which have served us in the past and serve us still, and scatter their members among the continents farthest from Europe . . . And to strip the halo of honor from political crimes, we shall put the culprits in the same dock as thieves, murderers, and other such vile and common criminals, thereby causing the public to associate political criminals with all others and despise them as they do all others.*' – p. 268.

20

In 1942, thirty-six years after Krushevan's articles first appeared in his Petersburg newspaper, a witness to the crime writes in his journal: 'I cannot comprehend the judicial basis for these murders – men killing one another quite openly, as though they were on stage.'

But the stage is real, as real as the corpses.

'They remain upright,' the wretched Kurt Gerstein writes, 'like basalt pillars; there is no space whatever to fall down or bend. Even in death, one can make out families holding hands. It is hard to separate them when the room must be cleared for the next load, blue bodies tossed out, soaked with sweat and urine, legs stained with excrement and menstrual blood. Two dozen workers check the mouths, prying them open with iron levers; others check the anus and genitals, looking for money, diamonds, gold. In the middle of it all stands Captain Wirth . . .'

In the middle of it all stands Captain Wirth. And in the upper left-hand pocket of his tunic is a leather-bound copy of *The Conspiracy* published by Der Hammer in 1933. He has read somewhere that the book saved the life of a young non-commissioned officer on the Russian front: a bullet fired from a sniper's rifle stuck in its pages, just above his heart. The book makes him feel safe.

Red Stamps with Lenin's Head

SONG OF SONGS, 8:6

Dear Sir,

In the course of your rue Michelet lecture you asked, 'What has become of Mendel Osipovich's correspondence?' and opined that the *Collected Works* published by Chekhov House in New York must be considered incomplete, that the correspondence might one day be found and will not therefore be limited to the twenty or so letters reproduced therein. After paying tribute to the labors of the tragically deceased Iosif Bezimensky ('It took thirty years of research to pick up the trail of people who, though they had not lost their lives, did lose their names, cities, countries, even continents'), you concluded there was still hope that the letters would surface and 'the irreparable would be repaired.'

I have been prompted to write to you by your incredible – incredibly audacious – conviction that the greater part of the correspondence still exists and that it is in the hands of an individual (I quote from memory) 'who for sentimental reasons or out of certain other considerations does not wish to part with these valuable documents.' It never entered my mind to ask you then, at the lecture, what it was that all of a sudden – because you expressed no such notion two years ago, nor did you mention anything of the sort in your preface – what it was that made you so certain as to state, 'The individual in question, if luck is with us, may still be alive somewhere in Berlin, Paris, or New York!' Your optimistic conclusion was doubtless based primarily on the research of the late Bezimensky and on his archives, to which you have had access.

The individual whom you seek, sir, 'the individual who holds the key to the mystery,' as you put it, was sitting several feet from you at the lecture. Of course you do not remember her; no doubt you did not even see her. And if you had happened to notice her, you would have thought she was one of those women who come to public lectures pretending they want to learn something – so that they may depart for the next world with their earthly obligations fulfilled and say at the end of the road that they did not live their lives in darkness – but who in fact come only to forget for a moment their own loneliness, filled as it is with thoughts of death, or simply to see another human being.

Despite the solitude I live in, sir, I do not plague others with my memories, which are peopled, like a huge graveyard, by the dead; I do not frequent lectures, nor do I write letters to strangers and occupy my time waiting for replies. Yet God is my witness – as now you shall be, too – that I have written a great many letters in my life. And nearly all of them were addressed to one and the same person: Mendel Osipovich.

You, a connoisseur of his work (it is not my intention to point out your biographical inaccuracies), have no need of lengthy explanations; you will easily find your bearings.

In the poem with the puzzling title 'Stellar Cannibalism' (Vol. I, p. 42), the 'meeting of two stars, two beings,' is by no means the 'product of a close collaboration between preconscious and subconscious activity,' as Miss Nina Roth-Swanson would have it; it is a poetic transposition of the electric shock that ran through Mendel Osipovich's soul the moment our eyes met in the offices of *Russkie zapiski* (he had called by 'accidentally and fatefully') in Paris on a gloomy November day in 1922. Likewise, M.O. did not, as the aforementioned lady claims, 'hymn his frustrations' in the émigré poems; he had always been what he himself called, though perhaps not without a tinge of irony, a 'poet of circumstance.'

I was twenty-three at the time. . . But I do not matter, I do not matter in the least. Let us return to Mendel Osipovich. In the poem 'Revelation,' from the same cycle, the 'cannibal stars' are neither 'subconscious fears connected with the poet's origins and with exile' nor 'the transposition of a nightmare,' and least of all 'totems'; they are the simple fusion of two images. On the day we met, Mendel Osipovich happened to have read an article in a popular-science magazine about stellar cannibalism, the phenomenon of double, *extremely close* stars (whence the line 'Stars that touch foreheads and chins') which swallow each other in clouds of mist somewhere on the far side of the Milky Way. That was the first stimulus. Our meeting was the second. The two events merged into a single image. And since poets speak as prophets, the poem about cannibal stars became prophetic: our lives, sir, commingled cannibalistically.

I had of course heard of Mendel Osipovich before I met him: all Yiddish speakers in Russia at the time – and not only Yiddish speakers – had heard of Mendel Osipovich. Like every powerful, original personality, he was surrounded by rumors: he was merely a cheap imitator of Ansky, he had an illegitimate child, he corresponded with a famous German actress, he had worn dentures since the age of eighteen (when a jealous husband, a well-known Russian poet, had knocked his teeth out), he wrote his poems in Russian first and then translated them with his father's help, he was preparing to move to Palestine, and so on. Once I saw a portrait of him by Pyotr Rotov in the newspapers. I immediately cut it out and pasted it in my diary thinking, Dear God, that's what the man of my life must look like! (Ah, the pathos of our youth.)

And suddenly – dear God! – there he was standing opposite me in the offices of *Russkie zapiski*, staring at me. I put my hands under the desk so he would not see them tremble.

The next day he took me to dinner at a Russian restaurant in Montparnasse. Since, according to a story circulating at the time, Mendel Osipovich, like Byron, felt utter contempt for women who ate in public, I ordered nothing, hungry though I was, but a cup of unsweetened tea. Later, of course, I told him of the consequences of the Byronic anecdote. The result was the famous 'anatomical poem', as Bezimensky calls it, in which 'after a celebration of the flesh, there appears, like a kid glove turned inside out, the idealized quintessence of the internal organs, not only the heart but also the lilac of the lungs and meanders of the gut.' It is therefore a love poem par excellence, not 'a series of fantasies about the maternal uterus'!

In a word, our love became 'inexorable and inescapable'; we realized that, in spite of all impediments, we had to join our lives. I shall not go into the obstacles standing in our way: families, clans, relatives, friends, the Writers' Organization. And of course that poor, sickly little girl, who was always held up as a last argument.

At his request I returned to Russia and found work in the Moscow offices of *Der Stern*. We could see each other every day. I lived very close to him, if not to say in his shadow. The poem 'Sun Beneath a Pink Lampshade' is Mendel Osipovich's ironic reply to a remark I made about this. (And not 'an obsession with menstrual blood', for goodness' sake!)

You are aware, sir, that M.O. was married at the time and had a daughter (or, as Nina Roth-Swanson writes, 'M.O. had incarnated his youthful fantasies in the person of a wife-mother'!). However painful it is for me, I must again remind you of the fate of that unfortunate child, whom Roth-Swanson ignores, as if the fact of her congenital illness might cast a shadow over Mendel Osipovich's life.

Far be it from me to emend the arbitrary assessments of the critics, least of all the analyses of Miss Nina Roth-Swanson – I have the *least* right to do so and the greatest – but there is one remark I feel I must make: N.R.-S., well aware of the sickly girl's existence, and out of feminine sympathy and, doubtless, a maternal instinct (which is not always relevant to critical assessment), interprets all poems in which the words *mayn kind* appear as 'anguish relating to the sanctions of the super-ego and experienced as a feeling of guilt'! Poor Mendel Osipovich would turn in his grave, if he read those words. Not only because of their revolting banality, though primarily for that reason, but also because never, sir, did M.O. make the slightest allusion to that child in his works: he would have considered it sacrilegious. *I*, sir, am the 'sinful parthenogenesis'; even though there was only a seven-year difference between us, *I* am the *mayn kind* of his poems. So much for the 'in-depth analysis' of Nina Roth-Swanson and her endeavor, on the basis of the novels *The Hounds* and *Pillar of Salt* as well as the volume of poems called *Falling Star*, to suggest the absurd thesis of love as incest, 'an attempt to violate taboos and experience catharsis as in a dream'! Forgive me, but the erudite Roth-Swanson would do well to spare Mendel Osipovich her 'totems and taboos.'

Need I tell you that M.O. often tried to break the bonds that kept him fettered 'on a double chain, like anchors.' But his unfortunate daughter, with an intuition given only to children and holy fools, was able to sense, the moment he stood in the doorway, his resolve to pronounce the fateful words he had recited on his way to her like a schoolboy on the way to an exam. Propped up on her pillows in bed, she would turn her mournful eyes to him and try to say something, which always ended in a terrifying, beast-like growl. M.O., tormented by remorse, would sit down next to her, take her hand in his, and, instead of launching into his prepared speech, bury his head in the lap of his wedded wife. 'God gave me this child along with my gift to keep me from growing proud,' he would repeat, sobbing.

Crushed, he fled back to literature, to 'The Promised Land.' (When I think of the misunderstandings and betrayals that poem caused him!) Then he would resolve to leave me. Like a sickly child or holy fool, I sensed his intentions by the ring of the doorbell, the turn of the key in the lock. 'Nobody needs to be hurt,' he would say. 'I have no right to love.' We parted many times 'for good,' snapping our bonds like a silver thread, 'the pearls rolling over yellowed, much scrubbed boards' (in my Merzlyakov Street walk-up apartment in Moscow), then falling immediately – 'inexorably' – back into each other's arms. (The poem 'Limbo' is nothing if not a response to those rifts.)

In the end – I say 'in the end,' for it took several years of suffering, of ruptures and separations – we realized that our lives were bound forever and that our feeble human powers were helpless against our love and against the obstacles in its path. 'Such a love is born once every three hundred years,' M.O. would say. 'It is the fruit of life, and life its only judge. Life and death.' That, then, is the meaning of 'Limbo,' a poem which, incidentally, Miss Nina Roth-Swanson's commentary reduces to utter nonsense. ('The image of the stream, the river, in the context of poetic speech, particularly when omitted, *suppressed*, derives from the dreamwork of the unconscious, and in dreams, by association, a flowing river, though invisible and merely sensed – a "resonant abyss" – suggests both the murmur of words and the splash of urine.' Now what is that gibberish supposed to mean?)

No, Mendel Osipovich never was my husband, but he was the meaning of my life, just as I was the 'cure for his grief' (see the twin poems 'The Prodigal Son' and 'Gaea and Aphrodite,' Vol. III, pp. 348–50). Ours was a love that needed none of the 'gluttonous joy of mortals,' that needed no proof; it nourished itself, consumed itself, but with a mutual flame.

And once the 'time of fiery ruptures' was past, we became captives, hostages to each other, and the temperature curve of our 'beautiful disease' grew steadier. I lost all 'dignity,' the last vestige of my upbringing. I no longer expected him to be anything but there, constant and solid as rock. I learned shorthand, the Guérin method, with a few additions of my own legible only to me. M.O. was at the peak of his fame at the time, which is to say much esteemed and much challenged; I was a young woman and still beautiful, a cause for much envy on the part of those who knew our secret. His feelings of guilt, the constant gnawings of his conscience, died down at last. During our years together, a 'time of cruelty and tenderness,' M.O. did his best work. (As for his biblical dramas, you must not forget, sir, that they contain dangerous allusions of the sort which, even if consigned to the drawer, could in those 'wolfish times' expose an author to mortal danger. Reading Miss Nina Roth-Swanson's commentaries – forgive me, but I bump into her at every turn as if she were a wardrobe placed in the middle of the room – and her interpretation of Moses as the personification of 'repressed hatred for the rabbi- and tyrant-father,' I wonder whether Nina R.-S. did not dream her way through the years she spent in Russia 'beneath the cruel skies of dear old Moses,' when instead of practicing 'in-depth analysis' she was a modest translator and lecturer.) I personally typed or copied out all Mendel Osipovich's works; I was, sir, the midwife to his literary labors (see, for example, the poem 'She said: "Amen,"' Vol. II, p. 94). For years I kept a suitcase packed, ready to leave at a word from him. I spent 'glorious nights of bestial fever' in infested provincial hotels and rented rooms. I remember – if I have the right to remember – the excitement we felt at our first merging in a Baku hotel: our clothes hung together in the wardrobe in lascivious intimacy. (I shall refrain from commenting on the interpretation Roth-Swanson gives the poem 'Merging Skins', overstepping, as it does, the bounds of decency and common sense.)

You may ask, sir, what all this has to do with Mendel Osipovich's oeuvre. Well, sir, I am the Polyhymnia in the poem of that name (and its meaning becomes clear only in the context of our experiences). 'In my every line, my every word, my every full stop I feel your presence like a drop of pollen,' M.O. used to say. 'Everything I have written, even everything I have translated, bears your mark.' He translated the Song of Songs in 1928; that is, at a time when the rifts between us belonged to the past. (Zanikovsky's contention that the translation is 'inaccurate' is ridiculous! The liberties M.O. took are justified by his own personal theory; there is no reason for Zanikovsky to bring in M.O.'s father, 'the highly regarded Yosef ben Bergelson,' and lay the blame on him. M.O. wove some of his personal feelings into these translations. 'How else, apart from sheer need, could I have derived such pleasure from translation?' he replied when I asked him about this. His versions of Catullus, Petrarch's *Canzoniere*, and Shakespeare's sonnets, which he prepared with the help of the late Izirkov, must also be read in this light.)

I shall pass over the historical events which like a harsh landscape provided the backdrop to our lives. When I look back, it all comes together in a mixture of snow, rain, and mud, in the 'unity of intolerable frost.' But you may rest assured, sir, that Mendel Osipovich had nothing of the stern mien his ascetic prose might suggest. The letters he wrote to me were as baroque as Flaubert's; they spoke of all the things his poetry speaks of – and of things it does not: creative joys and creative crises, innermost states, cities, hemorrhoids, landscapes, reasons to commit suicide and reasons to go on living, the difference between prose and poetry. His letters combined amorous sighs, erotic hints, literary theories, travelogues, and fragments of poetry. I still recall descriptions of a rose, of a sunrise, variations on the theme of bedbugs, speculations on the probability of life after death. I remember the description of a tree, a simile in which the crickets beneath a hotel window in the Crimea chirp like wristwatches being wound, the etymology of a name, of a city, the interpretation of a nightmare. The rest, everything else I can remember, was words of love: pointers on how to dress for the winter or comb my hair, prayers, 'ardent cooing,' and scenes of jealousy – unfounded, needless to say.

Then one day I received a letter. I need not tell you, sir, what happened in the terrible year of 1949, when every member of the Organization of Yiddish Writers was liquidated. The incident I am speaking of occurred just prior to those tragic events. I received a letter meant for another. Perhaps I ought to have subjected my curiosity to the rules of etiquette and left it unread, but that was too much to ask, especially since my name in Mendel Osipovich's hand was on the envelope. No, it was not a love letter; it was about the sense, the meaning of some verse – advice to the young woman who was translating Mendel Osipovich's poems into Russian. But the letter was permeated with a certain ambiguity, a mixture of 'Dionysian delirium' and 'incorrigible wood-grouse pride' (to quote from his verse itself). Mendel Osipovich's soul held no secrets for me. I was certain, sir, and still am (if certainty is not mere consolation or self-justification) that an ordinary *Liebesbrief* would have hurt me less, shaken me less: I could have forgiven him his 'Dionysian delirium'; in the name of our love, our unique, unrivaled love, I believe I could have forgiven him an infidelity of the flesh – with poets as with the gods, anything is forgivable. But the fact that he wrote to the young woman about his poetry, his soul, the mysterious sources of his inspiration; the fact that, in one ambiguous context proffered by the poetry itself, he shared with her something I felt belonged to me alone, and to him, a kind of *jus primae noctis* – that, sir, is what shattered me, shook my very being, and put all my erstwhile serenity to the test. All at once, in a disturbance of seismic proportions, the 'yellowed boards' opened beneath my feet and I began to flounder as one flounders in a nightmare. I realized that the only way I could stop my headlong fall was by taking decisive action, breaking a mirror, the lamp with the pink shade (that, too, a gift from him), a Chinese teapot, or a precious thermometer. Otherwise, I would have had to do something much more terrible. Then it occurred to me: the letters.

Because his apartment had been searched several times, Mendel Osipovich had moved our correspondence to mine. 'I fume at the idea of *faceless people* poking their noses into your letters,' he told me. I had tied the letters together with a black velvet ribbon he bought me when we first met. It appears in one of his poems, a poem in which enjambment stretches from line to line like a headband from temple to temple. From the moment I cut the ribbon with a pair of scissors that I found in my hand – I must have been intending to cut my hair – my fall went into slow motion. As soon as I tore the first letter, I knew I could not retreat, and this despite the realization running through me like a knife that I would regret my action, that I already regretted it. Our love was now like a precious novel with pages missing, like a defective copy one returns to a bookshop. So blinded was I by fury and remorse that I could make out nothing but a blur of stamps like a blob of red sealing wax. Since you are so at home in Mendel Osipovich's work, you must be wondering how *he* would have depicted the scene, this Flemish portrait with light streaming through the curtains onto the young woman's face and hands. For the sake of light, for the sake of the image, would he have lit a fire, fanned its flame, opened the doors of the stove? Would he have added a fireplace? (I had no fireplace, and the iron stove was out, even though it was March, icy March.) I don't believe so. A 'transparent twilight' is all he would have needed to illuminate the face of the woman by the window, and the red stamps with Lenin's head would have sufficed to highlight the red seal of 'imperial blood.' (The explanation you give of 'imperial blood' is perfectly valid.) Oh, he would have found a way to evoke the radiance of hell!

I could tell he had already discovered the fatal error. The moment he laid eyes on me, he knew what I was up to: there was a pile of shredded paper at my side. I stood up and thrust his books at him. 'I've torn out the inscriptions,' I said. Then I handed him an envelope full of photographs. 'I've destroyed the ones that showed us together.'

I saw him only once again – at a public meeting, reading a proclamation of some kind. He was a broken man by then; he sensed his end was near. You are aware of what followed. One night the 'faceless people' took him away and confiscated all the remaining letters. And that is how Mendel Osipovich's *Collected Works* were deprived of their fifth volume and his correspondence reduced to twenty notes to publishers and friends. What the terrible 'sword of the revolution' failed to destroy was destroyed by the frenzy of love.

What is done is done. The past lives on in us; we cannot erase it. Since dreams are an image of the otherworld and proof of its existence, we shall meet in dreams: he kneels by the stove, feeding it with damp wood, or calls to me in a hoarse voice. I wake up and switch on the light. Pain and remorse slowly turn into the melancholy joy of memories. Our long, passionate, terrible romance has filled my life and given it meaning. Fate has favored me, sir, and I seek no reparations. I shall not be in the index of Mendel Osipovich's books or in his biographies or in the footnotes to his poems. I, sir, am the very oeuvre of Mendel Osipovich, and he is mine. Is any fate more to be desired?

Please do not think, sir, that I have 'reconciled myself to my lot' and given up. Since no one knows where Mendel Osipovich lies buried, I have no intention of 'resting at his side' (as the unfortunate Z. has declared). If the arch-materialist Diderot could be carried away by such fantasies, why shouldn't I too, all materiality aside, hope that we shall meet in the other world? And I trust in God that I shall not find another shade at his side.

Postscript

All the stories in this book, to a greater or lesser extent, come under the sign of a theme I would call metaphysical: ever since the Gilgamesh epic, death has been one of the obsessive themes of literature. If the term 'divan' did not call for brighter hues and clearer tones, the collection might bear the subtitle The West-Easterly Divan *for its obvious ironic and parodic undercurrent.*

'Simon Magus' is a variation on the theme of one of the Gnostic legends. The Dictionnaire de Théologie catholique *cited by Jacques Lacarrière defines the Borborites as foul heretics*: 'Tertullian reproaches them for their lewdness and other sacrilegious wrongdoing. Clement of Alexandria says that they "wallow in lust like rams and douse their souls in the mire." The word "mire," *borboros*, is used to refer to these heretics because of their lewd habits . . . Did they in fact wallow in mire or is this merely a metaphor?'*

A well-intentioned and highly erudite individual has brought to my attention the similarity between Simon's schism, depicted in the story, and a passage written by Boris Souvarine in 1938! The passage reads as follows: 'Stalin and his subjects are always lying, at every opportunity, every minute, but because they never stop they no longer even realize they are lying. And

---

* Jacques Lacarrière, *Les Gnostiques* (Paris, 1973), p. 108.

when everyone lies, no one lies . . . The lie is a natural element of pseudo-Soviet society . . . The meetings, the congresses: theatricals, histrionics. The dictatorship of the proletariat: a patent fraud. The spontaneity of the masses: meticulous organization. The right, the left: lies. Stakhanov: a liar. The shockworker movement: a lie. The joyous life: a dismal farce. The new man: a grizzled gorilla. Culture: non-culture. The brilliant leader: a dull-witted tyrant . . .'* *Yet all similarity between the story and the passage cited is coincidental.*

The Jan Valtin in the story 'Last Respects' is a real person. In a large tome entitled Out of the Night *he refers to the episode as authentic, though the plot is highly reminiscent of so-called recurrent themes. The Flemish motifs are inspired by the atmosphere emanating from the canvases of Terborch, Rubens, and Rembrandt, by interpretations of them, and by the memory of a trip to Hamburg in 1972. The repulsive gladioluses, which O.V. had brought two or three days earlier, I painted from life, as, standing at the easel, one paints a* nature morte.†

'The Encyclopedia of the Dead' *was first published in* Književnost, *May – June 1981; a year later, on June 12, 1982, it appeared in* The New Yorker *in a translation by Ammiel Alcalay. The person who dreamed the dream and to whom the story*

---

* Alain Besançon, *Présence soviétique et passé russe* (Paris, 1980), pp. 278–79.

† The original title of this story was 'A Whore's Funeral.' The editor of one of our literary reviews informed me in a letter dated March 12, 1980, that 'the members of the editorial board have decided the title must be changed to the name of the heroine, "Mariette"' (which, as M. pointed out, makes a fine name for a whore but a poor title for a story). They had, it appears, taken a naïve, lyrical variation on a theme for a political allusion! (President Tito was gravely ill at the time. [Trans.]) The editor of another review, the Belgrade journal *Književnost* (*Literature*), relieved them of their headache by including the story in issue 8/1980. I changed the title myself for purely literary reasons: the original one had come to seem too literal.

is dedicated awoke one day to find, not without a shudder of amazement, that her most intimate nightmares were etched in stone, like a monstrous monument. About six months after the dream, and shortly after the story had appeared in print, a Yugoslav magazine published the following item under the title 'Archives':

East of Salt Lake City, the capital of the state of Utah, and deep in the Rockies' granite bowels, lies one of the most unusual archives in all the United States. It is reached by four tunnels blasted into the rock and consists of several underground rooms connected by a labyrinth of corridors. Access to the hundreds of thousands of microfilms stored there is limited to a highly select staff, and all entrances are equipped with iron doors and other security measures.

None of these measures is meant to protect top-secret information; the archives belong neither to the government nor to the military. They contain the names of eighteen billion people, living and dead, carefully entered on the 1,250,000 microfilms compiled to date by the Genealogical Society of the Church of the Latter-Day Saints. The Church was founded one hundred and fifty years ago by Joseph Smith and, according to Mormon sources, counts approximately three million adherents in the United States and an additional million abroad.

The names in these extraordinary archives come from all over the world; they have been copied painstakingly from the most varied records, and the work goes on. The ultimate goal of this stupendous undertaking is to enter on microfilm nothing less than the whole of mankind – not only the part that is still living but also the part that has passed on to the otherworld.

Genealogy is an essential element of religion for the Mormons. Thanks to the archives, every one of them can return to the past, retrace the family tree, and secure the retroactive baptism of those of their ancestors who were unfortunate enough to have missed the 'Mormon revelation.'

The Mormons take their task very seriously. The search for a suitable place to house the archives dates back to 1958, and drilling began three years later. The microfilms are preserved with the utmost care. The temperature in the subterranean facilities is maintained at forty degrees Fahrenheit; the humidity is between forty and fifty percent. The air is constantly circulated by a ventilation system and carefully filtered so as to prevent the slightest bit of dust or chemical pollution from entering the premises.

Six immense halls lined with a double layer of reinforced cement currently contain as much information as is contained in six million books of three thousand pages each.

Should it prove necessary, the Mormons are willing to construct new facilities. Every month, five to six miles of new microfilm arrive from all ends of the earth. Besides microfilms, the collection includes tens of thousands of books dealing directly or indirectly with genealogy, specialized periodical literature, works of history, etc.*

The legend of the seven sleepers of Ephesus clearly traces its origins to the Koran, but it was also recorded early in the sixth century by the Syrian writer Jacobus Sarguensis (De pueris Ephesi). Gregory of Tours (d. 594) agrees with Jacobus that the awakening represents one of the proofs of the Resurrection (De gloria confessum). Another variation on the theme of the resurrection of the dead occurs in the Talmud, in the Mishnah. There the sleeper awakens after seventy years. The legend has also been used by the Arab writer Tawfiq al-Hakim in a play entitled The Cave. It is al-Hakim, if I am not mistaken, who first introduced the figure of Prisca, the daughter of King Decius. Three hundred years later another Prisca, also a king's daughter, served as a kind of reincarnation of her namesake. The commentary in Jan Potocki's Manuscript Found in Saragossa

---

* *Duga* (*Rainbow*), May 19–23, 1981.

contains the following: 'The seven sleepers are seven noble Ephesian youths who, as legend has it, took refuge from Decius' persecution (the year was 250) in a cave on Mount Celius. Two hundred and thirty years later – 309 years later, according to other accounts – they awoke from their sleep, but died shortly thereafter. Their bodies were taken to Marseilles in a large stone coffin, which is now in the Eglise Saint-Victor. Their names were Constantine, Dionysius, John, Maximilian, Malchus, Martinian, and Serapion.'

The epigraph for my story comes from the eighteenth sura of the Koran, which is called 'The Cave': 'Some will say:/They were three and their dog the fourth;/Some will say:/They were five and their dog the sixth./Some will say, wishing to penetrate the mystery:/They were seven and their dog the eighth.' *As we can see, the number of sleepers is not the only mystery surrounding the legend. Denise Masson, referring to Muhammad Hamidullah, gives this explanation of the lines:* 'The nine years were added to establish an equilibrium between lunar and solar years.'

As for 'The Mirror of the Unknown,' it must be noted that spiritualists – including Madame Castellan herself – consider this fait divers *authentic. An analogous instance is cited by the celebrated astronomer Camille Flammarion (1842–1925), author of the equally celebrated* La Pluralité des mondes habités *and* Les Forces naturelles inconnues. *In his work* L'Inconnu et les problèmes psychiques *he alludes to the case of one Bérard, a former magistrate and member of the Assemblée nationale, who during an outing was forced to spend the night at a sordid inn 'in heavily wooded terrain.' In a dream that night Monsieur Bérard witnessed the detailed enactment of a murder that would take place three years later in the very room where he had slept the sleep of the just. The victim was a lawyer by the name of Victor Arnaud. It was thanks to Bérard's dream, which had* remained fresh in his memory, that the murderer was caught. The incident is also mentioned in the second volume of the memoirs of retired Police Inspector Garon, whose objectivity and lack of imagination are beyond question.*

'The Story of the Master and the Disciple' first appeared in Književna reč (The Literary Word) in the summer of 1976. It makes the farsighted but, from a psychological standpoint, wholly predictable point that the disciple would lead 'a long and merciless battle against him [the Master], "using gossip and slander in a manner that showed him to be not entirely without talent."' As time passes, the story loses more and more of its allegorical meaning, its center of gravity shifting in the direction of realism or even the documentary.†

'Pro Patria Mori' is a free reworking of a Late Bourgeois legend, a favorite of history-book writers and the subject of a number of variations – most recently in a book by a certain Frederic I-Gellé on the Black Hand – all of them based on Austrian sources not devoid of partiality, sesquipedality, and sentimentality.

'The Book of Kings and Fools' was originally conceived in the form of an essay, clear traces of which remain. My intention was to summarize the true and fantastic – 'unbelievably fantastic' – story of how The Protocols of the Elders of Zion came into existence, and to chronicle the work's insane impact on generations of readers and its tragic consequences. As a parable of evil, it has intrigued me for years (as is evident from certain passages in my novel Hourglass). I wanted to use a historically documented and more or less familiar case to cast doubt on the commonly accepted notion that books serve only good causes. In

* Yvonne Castellan, Le Spiritisme (Paris, 1954).
† Reference to a literary quarrel in Yugoslavia between September 1976 and March 1977, in which Kiš was accused of plagiarism by other writers including one, Branislav Šćepanović, whom Kiš had mentored. [Trans.]

point of fact, sacred books, and the canonized works of master thinkers, are like a snake's venom: they are a source of morality and iniquity, grace and transgression. 'Books in quantity are not dangerous; a single book is.'

The intended essay on The Protocols *fell apart the moment I tried to supplement it by imagining the parts of the book's history which have to this day remained obscure and will probably never be clarified; that is, when I felt the stirrings of that 'baroque need of the intelligence that drives it to fill every void' (Cortázar) and decided to bring to life characters who only lurked in the shadows – above all, the enigmatic Russian émigré whose name is Belogortsev in the story, and the even more enigmatic X, who, as the reader has seen, played a role of prime importance in unraveling the* Protocols *mystery. The essay lost its essayistic genre markings the moment I realized that in the domain of research, on the level of facts, there was no further progress to be made and I started imagining the events as they* might have happened. *It was then that with a clear conscience I changed the book's title from* The Protocols *to* The Conspiracy. *Begun on the fringe of the facts – and never betraying them entirely – the story took its own direction, where data were insufficient and facts unknown, in the penumbra where objects acquire shadows and outlines start to blur.*

To give the story a bit of drama, as Borges would say, I omitted some details and added others. 'When a writer calls his work a Romance,' *Nathaniel Hawthorne wrote,* 'it need hardly be observed that he wishes to claim a certain latitude, both as to its fashion and material.' *Needless to say, the statement applies perfectly to the short story as well.*

The informed reader will, I trust, have no trouble recognizing the famous Protocols *in* The Conspiracy *and will easily identify the figures concealed behind such designations as 'conspirators' and 'Satanic sects.' Of the enormous secondary literature on* The

Protocols *(which to a large extent rehashes the same material, with minor variations and additions but* different sympathies*), special mention should be made of studies by Norman Cohn** *and Ju. Delevsky and of* L'Apocalypse de notre temps *by Henry Rollin,*† *which is not only a basic research tool but also a moral or logical postscript to the tale: like a new victim of* The Conspiracy, *it was burned by German occupation forces in Paris. The astute reader will observe that several titles in Belogortsev's list bear on the topic as well.*

The reader may also be interested in the person of the 'unfortunate Kurt Gerstein,' who makes an appearance at the end of the story. This 'tragic hero of the German resistance' made the brave decision to join the SS *so as to sabotage its extermination policy from within.* 'As a result of his technical expertise he was appointed to the hygiene section of the Waffen-SS health services; that is, to the section assigned to perfecting poison gases in the guise of disinfectants. In the summer of 1942 he made a professional visit to the Belzec concentration camp ... He subsequently tried to galvanize world public opinion and succeeded in making contact with a Swedish diplomat, the Baron von Otter ... He also tried to obtain an audience with the papal nuncio in Berlin, but his request was denied ...' *His end was as tragic as it was absurd:* 'In May 1945 he was taken captive by French troops and incarcerated in Cherche-Midi Prison, where, alone and forlorn, he committed suicide in July of the same year' *(Léon Poliakov,* Bréviaire de la haine [*Paris, 1951*]).‡ *Gerstein wrote his testimony in French as a precautionary*

---

* *Warrant for Genocide: The Myth of the Jewish World Conspiracy and the Protocols of the Elders of Zion* (London, 1967). [Trans.]

† Paris: N.R.F., 1939. [Trans.]

‡ The passage quoted in the story is from p. 223. See also Helmut Krausnick, *Dokumentation zur Massenvergasung* (Bonn, 1956).

measure but also, surely, because Captain Wirth had made his native language repellent to him.

Despite its abundant quotations, the story 'Red Stamps with Lenin's Head' is pure fiction, although . . . although 'I never could understand,' *said Nabokov,* 'what was the good of thinking up books, of penning things that had not really happened in some way or other.'

The reference to the 'arch-materialist Diderot' derives doubtless from the following letter, which I discovered thanks to Madame Elisabeth de Fontenay: 'People who have loved each other in life and ask to be buried side by side are not perhaps so mad as is generally supposed. Perhaps their ashes press together, commingle, and unite . . . What do I know? Perhaps they have not lost all feeling, all memory of their original state; perhaps a remnant of warmth and life continues to smolder in them. O Sophie, if I might still hope to touch you, feel you, unite with you, merge with you when we are no more, if there were a law of affinity between our elements, if we were destined to form a single being, if in the train of centuries I were meant to become one with you, if the molecules of your moldering lover had the power to stir and move about and go in search of your molecules dispersed in nature! Leave me this wild fancy; it is so dear to me, it would ensure me an eternity in you and with you . . .'